A NIGHT IN
TERROR TOWER

Look for other **Goosebumps** books
by R.L. Stine

Goosebumps®

A NIGHT IN
TERROR TOWER

R.L. STINE

SCHOLASTIC INC.
New York Toronto London Auckland Sydney
Mexico City New Delhi Hong Kong Buenos Aires

21   7 8 9/0

Printed in the U.S.A.   40

First Scholastic printing, January 1995

"I'm scared," Eddie said.

I shivered and zipped my coat up to my chin. "Eddie, this was *your* idea," I told my brother. "I didn't beg and plead to see the Terror Tower. You did."

He raised his brown eyes to the tower. A strong gust of wind fluttered his dark brown hair. "I have a strange feeling about it, Sue. A bad feeling."

I made a disgusted face. "Eddie, you are such a wimp! You have a bad feeling about going to the movies!"

"Only *scary* movies," he mumbled.

"You're ten years old," I said sharply. "It's time to stop being scared of your own shadow. It's just an old castle with a tower," I said, gesturing toward it. "Hundreds of tourists come here every day."

"But they used to torture people here," Eddie said, suddenly looking very pale. "They used to lock people in the Tower and let them starve to death."

"Hundreds of years ago," I told him. "They don't torture people here anymore, Eddie. Now they just sell postcards."

We both gazed up at the gloomy old castle built of gray stones, darkened over time. Its two narrow towers rose up like two stiff arms at its sides.

Storm clouds hovered low over the dark towers. The bent old trees in the courtyard shivered in the wind. It didn't feel like spring. The air was heavy and cold. I felt a raindrop on my forehead. Then another on my cheek.

A perfect London day, I thought. A perfect day to visit the famous Terror Tower.

This was our first day in England, and Eddie and I had been sight-seeing all over London. Our parents had to be at a conference at our hotel. So they signed us up with a tour group, and off we went.

We toured the British Museum, walked through Harrods department store, visited Westminster Abbey and Trafalgar Square.

For lunch, we had bangers and mash (sausages and mashed potatoes) at a real English pub. Then the tour group took a great bus ride, sitting on top of a bright red double-decker bus.

London was just as I had imagined it. Big and crowded. Narrow streets lined with little shops and jammed with those old-fashioned—looking

2

black taxis. The sidewalks were filled with people from all over the world.

Of course my scaredy-cat brother was totally nervous about traveling around a strange city on our own. But I'm twelve and a lot less wimpy than he is. And I managed to keep him pretty calm.

I was totally surprised when Eddie begged to visit the Terror Tower.

Mr. Starkes, our bald, red-faced tour guide, gathered the group together on the sidewalk. There were about twelve of us, mostly old people. Eddie and I were the only kids.

Mr. Starkes gave us a choice. Another museum — or the Tower.

"The Tower! The Tower!" Eddie pleaded. "I've *got* to see the Terror Tower!"

We took a long bus ride to the outskirts of the city. The shops gave way to rows of tiny redbrick houses. Then we passed even older houses, hidden behind stooped trees and low, ivy-covered walls.

When the bus pulled to a stop, we climbed out and followed a narrow street made of bricks, worn smooth over the centuries. The street ended at a high wall. Behind the wall, the Terror Tower rose up darkly.

"Hurry, Sue!" Eddie tugged my sleeve. "We'll lose the group!"

"They'll wait for us," I told my brother. "Stop worrying, Eddie. We won't get lost."

We jogged over the old bricks and caught up

with the others. Wrapping his long, black over-coat around him, Mr. Starkes led the way through the entrance.

He stopped and pointed at a pile of gray stones in the large, grass-covered courtyard. "That wall was the original castle wall," he explained. "It was built by the Romans in about the year 400. London was a Roman city then."

Only a small section of the wall still stood. The rest had crumbled or fallen. I couldn't believe I was staring at a wall that was over fifteen hundred years old!

We followed Mr. Starkes along the path that led to the castle and its towers. "This was built by the Romans to be a walled fort," the tour guide told us. "After the Romans left, it became a prison. That started many years of cruelty and torture within these walls."

I pulled my little camera from my coat pocket and took a picture of the Roman wall. Then I turned and snapped a few pictures of the castle. The sky had darkened even more. I hoped the pictures would come out.

"This was London's first debtor prison," Mr. Starkes explained as he led the way. "If you were too poor to pay your bills, you were sent to prison. Which meant that you could *never* pay your bills! So you stayed in prison forever."

We passed a small guardhouse. It was about the size of a phone booth, made of white stones,

4

with a slanted roof. I thought it was empty. But to my surprise, a gray-uniformed guard stepped out of it, a rifle perched stiffly on his shoulder.

I turned back and gazed at the dark wall that surrounded the castle grounds. "Look, Eddie," I whispered. "You can't see any of the city outside the wall. It's as if we really stepped back in time."

He shivered. I don't know if it was because of my words or because of the sharp wind that blew through the old courtyard.

The castle cast a deep shadow over the path. Mr. Starkes led us up to a narrow entrance at the side. Then he stopped and turned back to the group.

I was startled by the tense, sorrowful expression on his face. "I am so sorry to give you this bad news," he said, his eyes moving slowly from one of us to the next.

"Huh? Bad news?" Eddie whispered, moving closer to me.

"You will all be imprisoned in the north tower," Mr. Starkes announced sternly. "There you will be tortured until you tell us the real reason why you chose to come here."

Eddie let out a startled cry. Other members of the tour group uttered shocked gasps.

Mr. Starkes began to chuckle as a grin spread over his round, red face. "Just a little Terror Tower joke," he said brightly. "I've got to have *some* fun, you know."

We all laughed, too. Except Eddie. He still seemed shaken. "That guy is crazy!" Eddie whispered.

Actually, Mr. Starkes was a very good tour guide. Very cheerful and helpful, and he seemed to know *everything* about London. My only problem was that sometimes I had trouble understanding his British accent.

"As you can see, the castle consists of several buildings," Mr. Starkes explained, turning serious. "That long, low building over there served as a barracks for the soldiers." He pointed across the broad lawn.

I snapped a picture of the old barracks. It looked

like a long, low hut. Then I turned and snapped a picture of the gray-uniformed guard standing at attention in front of the small guardhouse.

I heard several gasps of surprise behind me. Turning back, I saw a large hooded man creep out of the entrance and sneak up behind Mr. Starkes. He wore an ancient-looking green tunic and carried an enormous battle-ax.

An executioner!

He raised the battle-ax behind Mr. Starkes.

"Does anyone here need a very fast haircut?" Mr. Starkes asked casually, without turning around. "This is the castle barber!"

We all laughed. The man in the green executioner's costume took a quick bow, then disappeared back into the building.

"This is fun," Eddie whispered. But I noticed he was clinging very close to me.

"We are going to enter the torture chamber first," Mr. Starkes announced. "Please stick together." He raised a red pennant on a long stick. "I'll carry this high so you can find me easily. It's so easy to get lost inside. There are hundreds of chambers and secret passages."

"Wow. Cool!" I exclaimed.

Eddie glanced at me doubtfully.

"You're not too scared to go into the torture chamber, are you?" I asked him.

"Who? Me?" he replied shakily.

"You will see some very unusual torture devices," Mr. Starkes continued. "The wardens had many ways to inflict pain on their poor prisoners. We recommend that you do not try them at home."

A few people laughed. I couldn't wait to get inside.

"I ask you again to stick together," Mr. Starkes urged as the group began to file through the narrow doorway into the castle. "My last tour group was lost forever in there. Most of them are still wandering the dark chambers. My boss really scolded me when I got back to the office!"

I laughed at his lame joke. He had probably told it a thousand times.

At the entrance, I raised my eyes to the top of the dark tower. It was solid stone. No windows except for a tiny square one near the very top.

People were actually imprisoned here, I thought. Real people. Hundreds of years ago. I suddenly wondered if the castle was haunted.

I tried to read the serious expression on my brother's face. I wondered if Eddie was having the same chilling thoughts.

We stepped up to the dark entranceway. "Turn around, Eddie," I said. I took a step back and pulled my camera from my coat pocket.

"Let's go in," Eddie pleaded. "The others are getting ahead of us."

"I just want to take your picture at the castle entrance," I said.

I raised the camera to my eye. Eddie made a dumb face. I pressed the shutter release and snapped the picture.

I had no way of knowing that it was the last picture I would ever take of Eddie.

3

Mr. Starkes led the way down a narrow stairway. Our sneakers squeaked on the stone floor as we stepped into a large, dimly lit chamber.

I took a deep breath and waited for my eyes to adjust to the darkness. The air smelled old and dusty.

It was surprisingly warm inside. I unzipped my coat and pulled my long brown hair out from under the collar.

I could see several display cases against the wall. Mr. Starkes led the way to a large wooden structure in the center of the room. The group huddled closely around him.

"This is the Rack," he proclaimed, waving his red pennant at it.

"Wow. It's real!" I whispered to Eddie. I'd seen big torture devices like this in movies and comic books. But I never thought they really existed.

"The prisoner was forced to lie down here," Mr. Starkes continued. "His arms and legs were strapped down. When that big wheel was turned, the ropes pulled his arms and legs, stretching them tight." He pointed to the big wooden wheel.

"Turn the wheel more, and the ropes pulled tighter," Mr. Starkes said, his eyes twinkling merrily. "Sometimes the wheel was turned and the prisoner was stretched and stretched — until his bones were pulled right out of their sockets."

He chuckled. "I believe that is what is called doing a *long stretch* in prison!"

Some of the group members laughed at Mr. Starkes' joke. But Eddie and I exchanged solemn glances.

Staring at the long wooden contraption with its thick ropes and straps, I pictured someone lying there. I imagined the creak of the wheel turning. And the ropes pulling tighter and tighter.

Glancing up, my eye caught a dark figure standing on the other side of the Rack. He was very tall and very broad. Dressed in a long black cape, he had pulled a wide-brimmed hat down over his forehead, hiding most of his face in shadow.

His eyes glowed darkly out from the shadow.

Was he staring at me?

I poked Eddie. "See that man over there? The one in black?" I whispered. "Is he in our group?"

Eddie shook his head. "I've never seen him before," he whispered back. "He's weird! Why is he staring at us like that?"

The big man pulled the hat lower. His eyes

disappeared beneath the wide brim. His black cape swirled as he stepped back into the shadows.

Mr. Starkes continued to talk about the Rack. He asked if there were any volunteers to try it out. Everyone laughed.

I've got to get a picture of this thing, I decided. My friends will really think it's cool.

I reached into my coat pocket for my camera.

"Hey —!" I cried out in surprise.

I searched the other pocket. Then I searched my jeans pockets.

"I don't believe this!" I cried.

The camera was gone.

4

"Eddie — my camera!" I exclaimed. "Did you see —?"

I stopped when I saw the mischievous grin on my brother's face.

He held up his hand — with my camera in it — and his grin grew wider. "The Mad Pickpocket strikes again!" he declared.

"You took it from my pocket?" I wailed. I gave him a hard shove that sent him stumbling into the Rack.

He burst out laughing. Eddie thinks he's the world's greatest pickpocket. That's his hobby. Really. He practices all the time.

"Fastest hands on Earth!" he bragged, waving the camera at me.

I grabbed it away from him. "You're obnoxious," I told him.

I don't know why he enjoys being a thief so much. But he really is good at it. When he slid that camera from my coat pocket, I didn't feel a thing.

I started to tell him to keep his hands off my camera. But Mr. Starkes motioned for the group to follow him into the next room.

As Eddie and I hurried to keep up, I glimpsed at the man in the black cape. He was lumbering up behind us, his face still hidden under the wide brim of his hat.

I felt a stab of fear in my chest. Was the strange man watching Eddie and me? Why?

No. He was probably just another tourist visiting the Tower. So why did I have the frightening feeling he was following us?

I kept glancing back at him as Eddie and I studied the displays of torture devices in the next room. The man didn't seem interested in the displays at all. He kept near the wall, his black cape fading into the deep shadows, his eyes straight ahead — on us!

"Look at these!" Eddie urged, pushing me toward a display shelf. "What are these?"

"Thumbscrews," Mr. Starkes replied, stepping up behind us. He picked one up. "It looks like a ring," he explained. "See? It slides down over your thumb like this."

He slid the wide metal ring over his thumb. Then he raised his hand so we could see clearly. "There is a screw in the side of the ring. Turn the screw, and it digs its way into your thumb. Keep turning it, and it digs deeper and deeper."

"Ouch!" I declared.

"Very nasty," Mr. Starkes agreed, setting the thumbscrew back on the display shelf. "This is a whole room of very nasty items."

"I can't believe people were actually tortured with this stuff," Eddie murmured. His voice trembled. He really didn't like scary things — especially when they were real.

"Wish I had a pair of these to use on *you!*" I teased. Eddie is such a wimp. Sometimes I can't help myself. I have to give him a hard time.

I reached behind the rope barrier and picked up a pair of metal handcuffs. They were heavier than I imagined. And they had a jagged row of metal spikes all around on the inside.

"Sue — put those down!" Eddie whispered frantically.

I slipped one around my wrist. "See, Eddie, when you clamp it shut, the jagged spikes cut into your wrist," I told him.

I let out a startled gasp as the heavy metal cuff clicked shut.

"Ow!" I screamed, tugging frantically at it. "Eddie — help! I can't get it off! It's cutting me! It's cutting me!"

5

"Ohhhh." A horrified moan escaped Eddie's throat as he gaped at the cuff around my wrist. His mouth dropped open, and his chin started to quiver.

"Help me!" I wailed, thrashing my arm frantically, tugging at the chain. "Get me out of this!"

Eddie turned as white as a ghost.

I couldn't keep a straight face any longer. I started to laugh. And I slid the handcuff off my wrist.

"Gotcha back!" I jeered. "That's for stealing my camera. Now we're even!"

"I — I — I —" Eddie sputtered. His dark eyes glowered at me angrily. "I really thought you were hurt," he muttered. "Don't do that again, Sue. I mean it."

I stuck my tongue out at him. I know it wasn't very mature. My brother doesn't always bring out the best in me.

"Follow me, please!" Mr. Starkes' voice echoed off the stone walls. Eddie and I moved closer as our tour group huddled around Mr. Starkes.

"We're going to climb the stairs to the north tower now," the tour guide announced. "As you will see, the stairs are quite narrow and steep. So we will have to go single file. Please watch your step."

Mr. Starkes ducked his bald head as he led the way through a low, narrow doorway. Eddie and I were at the end of the line.

The stone stairs twisted up the Tower like a corkscrew. There was no handrailing. And the stairs were so steep and so twisty, I had to hold on to the wall to keep my balance as I climbed.

The air grew warmer as we made our way higher. So many feet had climbed these ancient stones, the stairs were worn smooth, the edges round.

I tried to imagine prisoners being marched up these stairs to the Tower. Their legs must have trembled with fear.

Up ahead, Eddie made his way slowly, peering up at the soot-covered stone walls. "It's too dark," he complained, turning back to me. "Hurry up, Sue. Don't get too far behind."

My coat brushed against the stone wall as I climbed. I'm pretty skinny, but the stairway was so narrow, I kept bumping the sides.

After climbing for what seemed like hours, we stopped on a landing. Straight ahead of us was a small dark cell behind metal bars.

"This is a cell in which political prisoners were held," Mr. Starkes told us. "Enemies of the king were brought here. You can see it was not the most comfortable place in the world."

Moving closer, I saw that the cell contained only a small stone bench and a wooden writing table.

"What happened to these prisoners?" a white-haired woman asked Mr. Starkes. "Did they stay in this cell for years and years?"

"No," Mr. Starkes replied, rubbing his chin. "Most of them were beheaded."

I felt a chill at the back of my neck. I stepped up to the bars and peered into the small cell.

Real people stood inside this cell, I thought. Real people held on to these bars and stared out. Sat at that little writing table. Paced back and forth in that narrow space. Waiting to meet their fate.

Swallowing hard, I glanced at my brother. I could see that he was just as horrified as I was.

"We have not reached the top of the Tower yet," Mr. Starkes announced. "Let us continue our climb."

The stone steps became steeper as we made our way up the curving stairway. I trailed my hand along the wall as I followed Eddie up to the top.

And as I climbed, I suddenly had the strangest

feeling — that I had been here before. That I had followed the twisting stairs. That I had climbed to the top of this ancient tower before.

Of course, that was impossible.

Eddie and I had never been to England before in our lives.

The feeling stayed with me as our tour group crowded into the tiny chamber at the top. Had I seen this tower in a movie? Had I seen pictures of it in a magazine?

Why did it look so familiar to me?

I shook my head hard, as if trying to shake away the strange, troubling thoughts. Then I stepped up beside Eddie and gazed around the tiny room.

A small round window high above our heads allowed a wash of gloomy gray light to filter down over us. The rounded walls were bare, lined with cracks and dark stains. The ceiling was low, so low that Mr. Starkes and some of the other adults had to duck their heads.

"Perhaps you can feel the sadness in this room," Mr. Starkes said softly.

We all huddled closer to hear him better. Eddie stared up at the window, his expression solemn.

"This is the tower room where a young prince and princess were brought," Mr. Starkes continued, speaking solemnly. "It was the early fifteenth century. The prince and princess — Edward and Susannah of York — were locked in this tiny tower cell."

19

He waved the red pennant in a circle. We all followed it, gazing around the small, cold room. "Imagine. Two children. Grabbed away from their home. Locked away in the drab chill of this cell in the top of a tower." Mr. Starkes' voice remained just above a whisper.

I suddenly felt cold. I zipped my coat back up. Eddie had his hands shoved deep in his jeans pockets. His eyes grew wide with fear as he gazed around the tiny, dark room.

"The prince and princess weren't up here for long," Mr. Starkes continued, lowering the pennant to his side. "That night while they slept, the Lord High Executioner and his men crept up the stairs. Their orders were to smother the two children. To keep the prince and princess from ever taking the throne."

Mr. Starkes shut his eyes and bowed his head. The silence in the room seemed to grow heavy.

No one moved. No one spoke.

The only sound was the whisper of wind through the tiny window above our heads.

I shut my eyes, too. I tried to picture a boy and a girl. Frightened and alone. Trying to sleep in this cold, stone room.

The door bursts open. Strange men break in. They don't say a word. They rush to smother the boy and girl.

Right in this room.

Right where I am standing now, I thought.

I opened my eyes. Eddie was gazing at me, his expression troubled. "This is . . . really scary," he whispered.

"Yeah," I agreed. Mr. Starkes started to tell us more.

But the camera fell out of my hand. It clattered noisily on the stone floor. I bent to pick it up. "Oh, look, Eddie — the lens broke!" I cried.

"Ssshhh! I missed what Mr. Starkes said about the prince and princess!" Eddie protested.

"But my camera —!" I shook it. I don't know why. It's not like shaking it would help fix the lens.

"What did he say? Did you hear?" Eddie demanded.

I shook my head. "Sorry. I missed it."

We walked over to a low cot against the wall. A three-legged wooden stool stood beside it. The only furniture in the chamber.

Did the prince and princess sit here? I wondered.

Did they stand on the bed and try to see out the window?

What did they talk about? Did they wonder what was going to happen to them? Did they talk about the fun things they would do when they were freed? When they returned home?

It was all so sad, so horribly sad.

I stepped up to the cot and rested my hand on it. It felt hard.

Black markings on the wall caught my eye. Writing?

Had the prince or the princess left a message on the wall?

I leaned over the cot and squinted at the markings.

No. No message. Just cracks in the stone.

"Sue — come on," Eddie urged. He tugged my arm.

"Okay, okay," I replied impatiently. I ran my hand over the cot again. It felt so lumpy and hard, so uncomfortable.

I gazed up at the window. The gray light had darkened to black. Dark as night out there.

The stone walls suddenly seemed to close in on me. I felt as if I were in a dark closet, a cold, frightening closet. I imagined the walls squeezing in, choking me, smothering me.

Is that how the prince and princess felt?

Was I feeling the same fear they had known over five hundred years ago?

With a heavy sigh, I let go of the cot and turned to Eddie. "Let's get out of here," I said in a trembling voice. "This room is just too frightening, too sad."

We turned away from the cot, took a few steps toward the stairs — and stopped.

"Hey —!" We both cried out in surprise.

Mr. Starkes and the tour group had disappeared.

6

"Where did they go?" Eddie cried in a shrill, startled voice. "They *left* us here!"

"They must be on their way back down the stairs," I told him. I gave him a gentle push. "Let's go."

Eddie lingered close to me. "You go first," he insisted quietly.

"You're not scared — are you?" I teased. "All alone in the Terror Tower?"

I don't know why I enjoy teasing my little brother so much. I *knew* he was scared. I was a little scared, too. But I couldn't help it.

As I said, Eddie doesn't always bring out the best in me.

I led the way to the twisting stairs. As I peered down, they seemed even darker and steeper.

"Why didn't we hear them leave?" Eddie demanded. "Why did they leave so fast?"

"It's late," I told him. "I think Mr. Starkes was eager to get everyone on the bus and back to their hotels. The Tower closes at five, I think." I glanced at my watch. It was five-twenty.

"Hurry," Eddie pleaded. "I don't want to be locked in. This place gives me the creeps."

"Me, too," I confessed.

Squinting into the darkness, I started down the steps. My sneakers slid on the smooth stone. Once again, I pressed one hand against the wall. It helped me keep my balance on the curving stairs.

"Where *are* they?" Eddie demanded nervously. "Why can't we hear the others on the stairs?"

The air grew cooler as we climbed lower. A pale yellow light washed over the landing just below us.

My hand swept through something soft and sticky. Cobwebs.

Yuck.

I could hear Eddie's rapid breathing behind me. "The bus will wait for us," I told him. "Just stay calm. Mr. Starkes won't drive off without us."

"*Is anybody down there?*" Eddie screamed. "*Can anybody hear me?*"

His shrill voice echoed down the narrow stone stairwell.

No reply.

"Where are the guards?" Eddie demanded.

"Eddie — please don't get worked up," I pleaded. "It's late. The guards are probably closing up. Mr. Starkes will be waiting for us down there. I promise you."

We stepped into the pale light of the landing.

The small cell we had seen before stood against the wall.

"Don't stop," Eddie pleaded, breathing hard. "Keep going, Sue. Hurry!"

I put my hand on his shoulder to calm him. "Eddie, we'll be fine," I said soothingly. "We're almost down to the ground."

"But, look — " Eddie protested. He pointed frantically.

I saw at once what was troubling him. There were *two* stairways leading down — one to the left of the cell, and one to the right.

"That's strange," I uttered, glancing from one to the other. "I don't remember a second stairway."

"Wh-which one is the right one?" he stammered.

I hesitated. "I'm not sure," I replied. I stepped over to the one on the right and peered down. I couldn't see very far because it curved so sharply.

"Which one? Which one?" Eddie repeated.

I don't think it matters," I told him. "I mean, they both lead *down* — right?"

I motioned for him to follow me. "Come on. I think this is the one we took when we were climbing up."

I took one step down.

Then stopped.

I heard footsteps. Heavy footsteps. Coming *up* the stairs.

Eddie grabbed my hand. "Who's that?" he whispered.

"Probably Mr. Starkes," I told him. "He must be coming back up to get us."

Eddie breathed a long sigh of relief.

"Mr. Starkes — is that you?" I called down.

Silence. Except for the approaching footsteps.

"Mr. Starkes?" I called in a tiny voice.

When the dark figure appeared on the stairway below, I could see at once that it wasn't our tour guide.

"Oh!" I uttered a startled cry as the huge man in the black cape stepped into view.

His face was still hidden in darkness. But his eyes glowed like burning coals as he glared up at Eddie and me from under the black, wide-brimmed hat.

"Is — is this the way down?" I stammered.

He didn't reply.

He didn't move. His eyes burned into mine.

I struggled to see his face. But he kept it hidden in the shadow of the hat, pulled low over his forehead.

I took a deep breath and tried again. "We got separated from our group," I said. "They must be waiting for us. Is — is this the way down?"

Again, he didn't reply. He glared up at us menacingly.

He's so big, I realized. He blocks the entire stairway.

"Sir — ?" I started. "My brother and I — "

He raised a hand. A huge hand, covered in a black glove.

He pointed up at us.

"You will come with me now," he growled.

I just stared at him. I didn't understand.

"You will come now," he repeated. "I do not want to hurt you. But if you try to escape, I will have no choice."

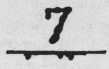

7

Eddie let out a sharp gasp.

My mouth dropped open as the man edged closer.

And then I realized who he was. "You're a guard here — right?" I asked.

He didn't reply.

"You — you scared me," I said, letting out a shrill laugh. "I mean, that costume and everything. You work here — right?"

He stepped forward, bringing his black-gloved hands up in front of him, moving the fingers.

"I'm sorry we're here so late," I continued. "We lost our group. I guess you want to close up so you can go home."

He took another step closer. His eyes flared darkly. "You know why I am here," he snarled.

"No. I don't. I —" My words were cut off as he grabbed me by the shoulder.

"Hey — let *go* of her!" Eddie cried.

But the caped man grabbed my brother, too.

His gloved fingers dug sharply into my shoulder. "Hey ___!" I cried out in pain.

He backed us against the cold stone wall.

I caught a glimpse of his face, a hard, angry face. A long, sharp nose, thin lips twisted in a snarl. And the eyes. The cold, glowing eyes.

"Let us go!" Eddie demanded bravely.

"We have to meet our group!" I told the man shrilly. "We're leaving now. You can't keep us here!"

He ignored our pleas. "Do not move," he uttered in a low growl. "Stand there. Do not try to escape."

"Listen, sir — if we've done something wrong . . ." My voice trailed off.

I watched him reach into the folds of his black cape. He struggled for a moment, then pulled something out.

At first I thought they were rubber balls. Three of them.

But as he clicked them together, I realized he was holding smooth, white stones.

What is going on here? I asked myself.

Is he crazy?

Crazy and dangerous?

"Listen, sir —" Eddie started. "We have to go now."

"Don't move!" the caped man screamed. He

shoved his cape violently behind him. "Don't move — and don't make a sound. You have my final warning!"

Eddie and I exchanged frightened glances. My back against the stone wall, I tried edging slowly toward the nearest stairway.

Mumbling to himself, the man concentrated on the three smooth white stones. He piled one on top of the other.

He let out an angry cry as one of the stones fell to the floor. It bounced once and slid across the smooth floor.

This is our chance! I thought.

I shoved Eddie toward the other stairwell. "Run!" I screamed.

"Do not move!" the man bellowed, grabbing up the stone. He had a booming voice that thundered off the stone walls. "I warned you. You cannot escape me!"

My brother's eyes were bugging out of his head. But he didn't have to be told twice to run!

"Stop!" the caped man bellowed. The booming voice followed us as we scrambled down, stumbling on the twisting, curving stairs, our hands trailing against the cold stone of the tower wall.

Down, down.

Turning so fast, my head spun. But I squinted into the dim light and forced myself not to be dizzy, not to fall, not to give in to the terror that rose up over me.

My camera fell out of my coat pocket. It clattered down the stairs. I didn't stop to pick it up. It was broken, anyway.

"Keep going," I urged Eddie. "Keep going! We're almost out of here!"

Or were we?

The climb down seemed so much longer.

Our sneakers slapped against the stone steps. But even louder were the heavy footsteps of the caped man behind us. His bellowed cries boomed down the narrow tower, echoed all around us — as if we were being chased by a *hundred* frightening men instead of one.

Who is he?

Why is he chasing us?

Why is he so angry?

The questions bounced through my mind as I scrambled frantically down, following the twisting stairs.

No time for answers.

The big, gray door rose up in front of us before we could stop.

Eddie and I both ran right into it.

"The exit! We — we're here!" I stammered. I could hear the rumble of the man's footsteps above us on the stairway. Coming closer. Closer.

We're out! I thought. *We're safe!*

Eddie shoved the door hard with his shoulder. Shoved it again.

He turned to me, his chin quivering in fright. "It's locked. We're locked in!"

"No!" I screamed. "Push!"

We both lowered our shoulders and pushed with all our strength.

No.

The door didn't budge.

The man lumbered closer. So close, we could hear his muttered words.

We're trapped, I realized.

He's caught us.

Why does he want us? What is he going to do?

"One more try," I managed to choke out.

Eddie and I turned back to the door.

"Stay there!" the caped man commanded.

But Eddie and I gave the door one more desperate shove.

And it finally moved, scraping the stone floor as it slid open partway.

Eddie sucked in his breath and pushed through the opening first. Then I squeezed through.

Panting hard, we shoved the door shut behind us. The door had a long metal bar on the outside. I slid it all the way, bolting it. Locking the caped man inside.

"We're safe!" I cried, spinning away from the door.

But we weren't outside. We were in a huge, dark room.

And a cruel voice — in the room with us — a man's voice, laughing softly — told me that we weren't out of trouble.

9

The laughter rose up in front of us, making us both gasp.

"You have entered the king's dungeon. Abandon all hope," the man declared.

"Who — who are you?" I cried.

But more laughter was the only reply.

A single beam of pale green light from the low ceiling broke the darkness. Huddled close to Eddie, I squinted in the eerie glow, desperate to find a way to escape.

"Over there! Look!" Eddie whispered, pointing.

Across the room, I could see a barred cell against the wall.

We crept forward a few steps. Then we saw it.

A bony hand reaching out from between the bars.

"No!" I gasped.

Eddie and I jumped back.

The pounding on the door behind us made us

both jump again. "You cannot escape!" the caped man raged from the other side of the door.

Eddie grabbed my hand as the man furiously pounded on the door. The sound boomed louder than thunder.

Would the bolt hold?

Ahead of us, two bony hands reached out from another dungeon cell.

"This can't be happening!" Eddie choked out. "There aren't any dungeons today!"

"Another doorway!" I whispered, trembling with fright as I stared at the hands poking out from the dark cells. "Find another doorway."

My eyes frantically searched the darkness. Off in a distant corner, I glimpsed a slender crack of light.

I started to run toward it — and tripped over something. Something chained to the floor.

It was a body. A body of a man sprawled on the floor. And I landed on his chest with a sickening *thud*.

The chains rattled loudly as my foot tangled in them.

My knees and elbows hit the stone floor hard. Pain shot through my entire body.

The old man didn't move.

I scrambled up. Stared down at him.

And realized he was a dummy.

Not real. Just a dummy, chained to the floor.

"Eddie — it's not real!" I cried.

"Huh?" He stared at me, his face twisted in confusion, in fright.

"It's not real! None of it!" I repeated. "Look! The hands in the dungeon cells — they're not moving! It's all a display, Eddie. Just a display!"

Eddie started to reply. But the cruel laughter interrupted him.

"You have entered the king's dungeon. Abandon all hope," the voice repeated. Then more evil laughter.

Just a tape. Just a recording.

There wasn't anyone in the room with us. No dungeon keeper.

I let out a long sigh. My heart was still pounding like a bass drum. But I felt a little better knowing that we weren't trapped in a real dungeon.

"We're okay," I assured Eddie.

And then the door burst open with a loud *crack*. And the big man roared into the room, his cape fluttering behind him, his dark eyes glowing in victory.

10

Eddie and I froze in the middle of the floor.

The caped man froze, too. The only sound was his harsh, raspy breathing.

We stared through the dim light at each other. Frozen like the dummies in the cells.

"You cannot escape," the man growled once again. "You know you will not leave the castle."

His words sent a cold shiver down my back.

"Leave us alone!" Eddie pleaded in a tiny voice.

"What do you want?" I demanded. "Why are you chasing us?"

The big man pressed his gloved hands against his waist. "You know the answer," he replied flatly. He took a step toward Eddie and me. "Are you ready to come with me now?" he demanded.

I didn't reply. Instead, I leaned close to Eddie and whispered, "Get ready to run."

Eddie continued to stare straight ahead. He didn't blink or nod his head. I couldn't tell if he had even heard me.

"You know you have no choice," the man said softly. He reached both hands into the folds of his cape. Once again, he pulled out the mysterious white stones. And once again, I caught a glimpse of his dark eyes, saw the cold sneer on his lips.

"You — you've made a mistake!" Eddie stammered.

The man shook his head. The wide brim of the black hat cast tilting shadows on the floor. "I have made no mistake. Do not run from me again. You know you must come with me now."

Eddie and I didn't need a signal.

Without saying a word to each other, without *glancing* at each other, we spun around — and started to run.

The man shouted in protest and took off after us.

The room seemed to stretch on forever. It must be the entire basement of the castle, I realized.

Beyond the beam of light, the darkness rose up like fog.

My fear weighed me down. My legs felt as if they were a thousand pounds each.

I'm moving in slow motion, I thought, struggling to speed up. Eddie and I are crawling like turtles.

He'll catch us. He'll catch us in two seconds.

I glanced back when I heard the caped man cry out. He had tripped over the same dummy chained to the floor. He had fallen heavily.

As he scrambled to his feet, my eyes searched the far wall for a door. Or a hallway. Or any kind of opening.

"How — how do we get *out* of here?" Eddie cried. "We're trapped, Sue!"

"No!" I cried. I spotted a worktable against the wall. Cluttered with tools. I searched for something to use as a weapon. Didn't see anything. Grabbed a flashlight, instead.

Frantically pushed the button.

Would it work?

Yes.

A white beam of light darted over the floor. I raised it to the far wall. "Eddie — look!" I whispered.

A low opening in the wall. Some kind of tunnel? A tunnel we could escape through?

In another second, we were ducking our heads and stepping into the dark opening.

I kept my light ahead of us, down at our feet. We had to stoop as we ran. The tunnel was curved at the top, and not high enough for us to stand.

The tunnel ran straight for a while, then curved down and to the right. The air felt damp and cool. I could hear the trickle of water nearby.

"It's an old sewer," I told Eddie. "That means it has to lead us out somewhere."

"I hope so," Eddie replied breathlessly.

Running hard, we followed the curve of the

sewer. My light leaped about, jumping from the low ceiling to the damp stone floor.

The light revealed wide metal rungs hanging from the ceiling. Eddie and I had to duck even lower to keep from smashing our heads against them.

The light from my flashlight bounced wildly from the floor to the rungs along the top of the sewer. Eddie and I splashed through puddles of dirty water.

We both gasped when we heard the footsteps behind us.

Heavy, ringing footsteps. Thundering in the low tunnel. Growing louder. Louder.

I glanced back. But the caped man was hidden by the curve of the sewer tunnel.

His footsteps boomed steadily, rapidly. I could tell he wasn't far behind.

He's going to catch us, I told myself in a panic.

This tunnel is never going to end.

Eddie and I can't run much farther.

He's going to catch us in this dark, damp sewer. And then what?

What does he want?

Why did he say that we *knew* what he wanted?

How could we know?

I stumbled forward. The flashlight bumped against the wall and fell from my hand.

It clattered to the tunnel floor and rolled in front of me.

The light shone back into the tunnel, back toward the caped man.

I saw him move into view, bent low, running hard.

"Ohhh." A frightened moan escaped my lips.

I bent to pick up the flashlight. It slid out of my trembling hand.

That was all the time the caped man needed.

He grabbed Eddie with both hands. He pulled the black cape around my brother, trapping him.

Then he reached for me. "I told you — there is no escape," he rasped.

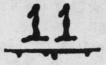

I ducked out of the caped man's grasp.

With another frightened groan, I grabbed the flashlight off the floor.

I planned to use it as a weapon. To shine it in the caped man's eyes. Or swing it at his head.

But I didn't get a chance.

I froze in horror as the beam of light bounced down the tunnel — and I saw the rats.

Hundreds of them. Hundreds of chittering gray rats.

The darting light made their eyes glow red as fire. The rats came scrabbling over the sewer floor. Snapping their jaws hungrily, gnashing their jagged teeth as they came charging at us.

Their shrill whistling and chittering echoed through the tunnel. The terrifying sound made my breath catch in my throat.

The tiny red eyes glowed in the light as they scrabbled toward us. As they pulled their scrawny bodies over the hard floor, their tails slithered behind them like dark snakes.

The caped man saw them, too. He leaped back in surprise.

And Eddie came tearing out from under the cape. He gulped in shock as his eyes locked on the charging rats.

"Jump!" I cried. "Eddie — jump!"

Eddie didn't move. We both gaped at the rats in horror. A churning sea of whistling, chewing, red-eyed rats. A living tidal wave of rats.

"Jump! Jump — now!" I shrieked.

I raised both hands. Jumped.

Eddie jumped, too. We grabbed on to the metal bars imbedded in the sewer roof.

Pulling myself up, I frantically lifted my feet as high as I could from the floor.

Higher. Higher. As the rats charged underneath me.

A foul odor rose up, nearly choking me as the rats ran past.

I could hear the *tap tap tap* of their long toenails against the floor. Hear the *swish* of their sweeping tails.

I couldn't see the rats in the darkness. But I could hear them. And feel them. They jumped at my shoes. Scratched at my legs with their sharp claws. And kept coming.

I turned to see the caped man start to run back.

He stumbled with lurching steps as he tried to flee the thundering wave of rats. His arms shot forward as if reaching for safety. The black cape whipped up behind him.

The wide-brimmed hat flew off his head and floated to the floor. A dozen rats pounced on it, climbed all over it, and began chewing it to pieces.

The man's footsteps echoed in the tunnel as he ran faster. Rats leaped up at his cape, clawing it, snapping their jaws, and shrieking excitedly.

A second later, he disappeared around the curve of the sewer.

The rats scrambled noisily after him. As they vanished around the curve, the sounds all blended together, became a roar, a roar that rang through the long sewer.

A roar of horror.

My arms were both aching, throbbing with pain. But I kept my feet high off the floor. I didn't let go of the metal rung until I was sure all the rats had disappeared.

The roar faded into the distance.

I heard Eddie's heavy breathing. He let out a sharp groan and dropped to the floor.

I let go of the bar and lowered myself, too. I waited for my heart to stop pounding, for the blood to stop throbbing at my temples.

"That was a close call," Eddie murmured. His chin trembled. His face was as gray as the tunnel walls.

I shuddered. I knew I'd see the hundreds of tiny red eyes in my dreams, hear the clicking of their long toenails and the *swish* of their scraggly tails.

"Let's get out of this disgusting sewer!" I cried. "Mr. Starkes must be frantic searching for us."

Eddie picked up the flashlight and handed it to me. "I can't wait to get back on the tour bus," he said. "I can't wait to get away from this awful tower. I can't believe we've been chased by a crazy person through a sewer. This can't really be happening to us, Sue!"

"It's happening," I declared, shaking my head. I suddenly had another thought. "Mom and Dad are probably out of their meeting," I said. "They're probably worried sick about us."

"Not as worried as I am!" Eddie exclaimed.

I beamed the light ahead, keeping it down on the sewer floor, and we started walking. The tunnel floor rose up and curved to the left. We started to climb.

"There's *got* to be an end to this sewer," I muttered. "It's *got* to end somewhere!"

A faint roar up ahead made me cry out.

More rats!

Eddie and I both stopped. And listened.

"Hey —!" I uttered excitedly when I realized it was a different sound.

The sound of wind rushing into the tunnel.

That meant we had to be close to the end. And that the sewer emptied somewhere *outside*.

"Let's go!" I cried excitedly. The beam of light bounced ahead of us as we started to run.

The tunnel curved again. And then suddenly ended.

I saw a metal ladder, reaching straight up. Straight up to a large, round hole in the tunnel ceiling. Gazing up at the hole, I saw the night sky.

Eddie and I let out shouts of joy. He scrambled up the ladder, and I pulled myself up right behind him.

It was a cold, damp night. But we didn't care. The air smelled so fresh and clean.

And we were out. Out of the sewer. Out of the Terror Tower.

Away from that frightening man in the black cape.

I gazed around quickly, trying to figure out where we were. The Tower tilted up toward us, a black shadow against the blue-black sky.

The lights had all been turned off. The tiny guardhouse lay dark and empty. Not another soul in sight.

I saw the low wall that divided the Tower from the rest of the world. And then I found the stone path that led to the exit and the parking lot.

Our shoes thudded over the smooth stones as we hurried toward the parking lot. A pale half-moon slid out from behind wispy clouds. It cast a shimmering silver light over the whispering trees and the long stone wall.

It all suddenly looked unreal.

Without stopping, I glanced back at the old castle. The moonlight shone off the jutting towers, as if casting them in a pale spotlight.

Real people walked on this path hundreds of years ago, I thought.

And real people died up in that tower.

With a shiver, I turned back and kept jogging. Eddie and I moved through the open gate and out past the wall.

We're back in modern times, I thought. Back where we are safe.

But our happiness didn't last long.

The parking lot shimmered darkly in the pale moonlight. Empty.

The tour bus was gone.

Eddie and I both turned to search up and down the street. The long, empty street.

"They left us," Eddie murmured with a sigh. "How are we going to get back to the hotel?"

I started to answer — but stopped when I saw the man.

A tall, white-haired man, limping toward us, moving fast, pointing and calling, "You there! You there!"

Oh, no, I thought wearily, feeling my body freeze in fear.

Now what?

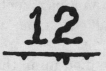

12

"You there! You there!"

The man's shoulder dipped in the big, gray over-coat he wore as he charged at us, limping with each step.

Eddie and I huddled close together, staring back at him as he hurried across the empty parking lot. His white hair tumbled out from under a small gray cap. The overcoat hung down nearly to his ankles and bulged over his skinny frame.

He stepped up in front of us and waited to catch his breath. His tiny eyes caught the moonlight as he narrowed them at us, studying Eddie, then me.

"Are you the two kids that bus driver was looking for?" he asked in a shrill, high voice. He had a different accent from Mr. Starkes'. I think it was Scottish.

Eddie and I nodded.

"Well, I'm the night guard here," the man told us. "There's no one here but me after closing."

"Uh . . . where is our bus?" Eddie asked quietly.

"It left," the man replied sharply. "He searched all over for you. But he couldn't wait any longer. What happened? Did you get lost in there?" He motioned back toward the Tower.

"A man chased us," Eddie replied breathlessly. "He said we had to come with him. He was really scary, and —"

"Man? What man?" The night guard eyed us suspiciously.

"The man in the black cape!" I replied. "And the black hat. He chased us. In the Tower."

"There's no man in the tower," the guard replied, shaking his head. "I told you. I'm the only one here after closing."

"But he's in there!" I cried. "He chased us! He was going to hurt us! He chased us through the sewer and the rats —"

"Sewer? What were you two doing in the sewer?" the guard demanded. "We have rules here about where tourists are allowed. If you break the rules, we can't be responsible."

He sighed. "Now you come out here with a wild story about a man in a black cape. And running through the sewers. Wild stories. Wild stories."

Eddie and I exchanged glances. We could both see that this man wasn't going to believe us.

"How do we get back to our hotel?" Eddie asked. "Our parents will be really worried."

49

I glanced at the street. There were no cars or buses in sight.

"Do you have any money?" the guard asked, replacing his cap. "There's a phone box on the corner. I can call for a taxi."

I reached into my jeans pocket and felt the heavy coins my parents had given me before Eddie and I set out on the tour. Then I breathed a long sigh of relief.

"We have money," I told the guard.

"It'll cost you at least fifteen or twenty pounds from way out here," he warned.

"That's okay," I replied. "Our parents gave us British money. If we don't have enough, my parents will pay the driver."

He nodded. Then he turned to Eddie. "You look all done in, lad. Did you get frightened up in that tower?"

Eddie swallowed hard. "I just want to get back to our hotel," he murmured.

The guard nodded. Then, tucking his hands into the pockets of the big overcoat, he led the way to the phone booth.

The black taxi pulled up about ten minutes later. The driver was a young man with long, wavy blond hair. "What hotel?" he asked, leaning out the passenger window.

"The Barclay," I told him.

Eddie and I climbed into the back. It was warm in the taxi. It felt so great to sit down!

As we pulled away from the Terror Tower, I didn't glance back. I never wanted to see that old castle again.

The car rolled smoothly through the dark streets. The taxi meter clicked pleasantly. The driver hummed to himself.

I shut my eyes and leaned my head back against the leather seat. I tried not to think about the frightening man who had chased us in the Tower. But I couldn't force him from my mind.

Soon we were back in the center of London. Cars and taxis jammed the streets. We passed brightly lit theaters and restaurants.

The taxi pulled up to the front of the Barclay Hotel and eased to a stop. The driver slid open the window behind his seat and turned to me. "That'll be fifteen pounds, sixty pence."

Eddie sat up drowsily. He blinked several times, surprised to see that we had reached our destination.

I pulled the big, heavy coins from my pocket. I held them up to the driver. "I don't really know what is what," I confessed. "Can you take the right amount from these?"

The driver glanced at the coins in my hands, sniffed, then raised his eyes to me. "What are those?" he asked coldly.

"Coins," I replied. I didn't know what else to say. "Do I have enough to pay you?"

He stared back at me. "Do you have any *real* money? Or are you going to pay me with play money?"

"I — I don't understand," I stammered. My hand started to tremble, and I nearly dropped the coins.

"I don't either," the driver replied sharply. "But I do know that those aren't real coins. We use British pounds here, miss."

His expression turned angry. He glared at me through the little window in the glass partition. "Now, are you going to pay me in British pounds, or are we going to have some major trouble? I want my money — now!"

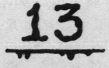

13

I pulled the coins away from him and raised them close to my face. It was dark in the back of the taxi, and hard to see.

The coins were large and round. They felt heavy, made of real gold or silver. It was too dark to read the words on them.

"Why would my parents give me play money?" I asked the driver.

He shrugged. "I don't know your parents."

"Well, they will pay you the fifteen pounds," I told him. I struggled to shove the big coins back into my pocket.

"Fifteen pounds, sixty — plus tip," the driver said, frowning at me. "Where are your parents? In the hotel?"

I nodded. "Yes. They were at a meeting in the hotel. But they're probably up in the room now. We'll get them to come down and pay you."

"In real money, if you please," the driver said,

rolling his eyes. "If they're not down here in five minutes, I'll come in after you."

"They'll be right down. I promise," I told him.

I pushed open the door and scrambled out of the cab. Eddie followed me onto the sidewalk, shaking his head. "This is weird," he muttered.

A red-uniformed doorman held the hotel door open for us, and we hurried into the huge, chandeliered lobby. Most people seemed to be heading the other way, going out for dinner, I guessed.

My stomach grumbled. I suddenly realized I was starving.

Eddie and I made our way past the long front desk. We were walking so fast, we nearly collided with a bellman pushing a big cart stacked high with suitcases.

To our right, I could hear dishes clattering in the hotel restaurant. The aroma of fresh-baked bread floated in the air.

The elevator doors opened. A red-haired woman in a fur coat stepped off, walking a white toy poodle. Eddie got tangled in the leash. I had to pull him free so we wouldn't miss the elevator.

We stumbled into the elevator. As the doors slid shut, I pushed Six. "What was wrong with that money?" Eddie asked.

I shrugged. "I don't know. I guess Dad made a mistake."

The doors slid open on six, and we hurried side

by side down the long, carpeted hall to our room.

I stepped around a room service tray on the floor. Someone had left half a sandwich and part of a bowl of fruit. My stomach rumbled again, reminding me how hungry I was.

"Here we are." Eddie ran up to the door to room 626 and knocked. "Hey, Mom! Dad! It's us!"

"Open up!" I called impatiently.

Eddie knocked again, a little louder. "Hey —!"

We pressed our ears close to the door and listened.

Silence. No footsteps. No voices.

"Hey — are you in there?" Eddie called. He knocked again. "Hurry up! It's us!"

He turned to me. "They *must* be out of that meeting by now," he muttered.

I cupped my hands around my mouth. "Mom? Dad? Are you there?" I called in.

No reply.

Eddie's shoulders slumped, and he let out an unhappy sigh. "Now what?"

"Are you having trouble?" a woman's voice asked.

I turned to see a hotel maid. She wore a gray uniform and a small white cap over her short, dark hair. She had been pushing a cart loaded with towels. She stopped across from Eddie and me.

"Our parents are still at a meeting," I told her. "My brother and I — we're locked out."

She studied us for a moment. Then she stepped away from the cart and raised a large keychain filled with keys.

"I'm not really supposed to do this," she said, shuffling through the clattering keys. "But I guess it's okay to let you kids in."

She put a key into the lock, turned it, and pushed open the door for us. Eddie and I both thanked her and told her she was a lifesaver. She smiled and moved on down the hall, pushing her towel cart.

The room was dark. I clicked on the light as Eddie and I stepped in.

"They're not here," I said softly. "No sign of them."

"They probably left a note," Eddie replied. "Maybe they had to go out with people from the meeting. Or maybe they're down in the restaurant, waiting for us."

Our room was actually a suite. A front room and two bedrooms.

Turning on lights as I went, I made my way to the desk in the corner. A writing pad and pen rested in the center of the desk. But the pad was blank. No message.

No message from Mom or Dad on the bedtable, either.

"That's weird," Eddie muttered.

I crossed the room and stepped into their bedroom. I clicked on the ceiling light and glanced around.

The room had been made up. The bed was smooth and unwrinkled. There was no message for us anywhere. The dressertop lay bare. No clothes tossed over a chair. No shoes on the floor. No briefcases or notepads from their meeting.

No sign that anyone had even been in the room.

I turned and saw that Eddie had moved to the closet. He pushed the sliding door open all the way.

"Sue, look!" he shouted. "No clothes! Mom's and Dad's clothes — our clothes — they're all gone!"

A heavy feeling of dread started in my stomach and weighted down my entire body. "What is going *on* here?" I cried.

14

"They wouldn't just leave!" I exclaimed. I walked over to the closet and checked it out for myself. I don't know what I expected to see. It was clear from across the room that the closet was completely empty.

"Are you sure we're in the right room?" Eddie asked. He pulled open the top dresser drawer. Empty.

"Of course this is the right room," I replied impatiently.

Eddie pulled out the rest of the dresser drawers. They were all empty.

We searched every inch of the room. No sign of Mom or Dad.

"We'd better go down to the desk," I suggested, thinking hard. "We'll find out what room the meeting is being held in. Then we'll go there and talk to Mom and Dad."

"I can't believe they're still at the meeting,"

Eddie murmured, shaking his head. "And why would they pack up and take all our clothes to the meeting with them?"

"I'm sure there's a good answer," I said. "Come on. Let's go downstairs."

We made our way back down the long hall and took the elevator to the lobby.

We found a crowd around the front desk. A large woman, dressed in a green pantsuit, was arguing angrily about her room. "I was promised a view of the river," she screamed at the red-faced man behind the desk. "And I want a view of the river!"

"But, madam," he replied softly, "the hotel is not located near the river. We do not have any river views from this hotel."

"I must have a river view!" the woman insisted. "I have it right here in writing!" She flashed a sheet of paper in front of the man's face.

The argument continued for a few minutes more. I quickly lost interest in it. I thought about Mom and Dad. I wondered where they were. I wondered why they hadn't left us a note or a message.

Eddie and I finally got up to the desk about ten minutes later. The clerk tucked some papers into a file, then turned to us with an automatic smile. "Can I help you?"

"We're trying to find our parents," I said, leaning my elbows on the desk. "They're in the meeting, I think. Can you tell us where the meeting is?"

He stared at me for a long moment, his face blank, as if he didn't understand. "What meeting is that?" he asked finally.

I thought hard. I couldn't remember what the meeting was called. Or what it was about.

"It's the big meeting," I replied uncertainly. "The one people came from all over the world for."

He twisted his mouth into a thoughtful pout. "Hmmm . . ."

"A very big meeting," Eddie chimed in.

"We have a problem," the clerk said, frowning. He scratched his right ear. "There aren't any meetings in the hotel this week."

I stared back at him. My mouth dropped open. I started to say something, but the words just didn't come out.

"No meetings?" Eddie asked weakly.

The clerk shook his head. "No meetings."

A young woman called to him from the office. He signaled to me that he'd be right back. Then he hurried over to see what she wanted.

"Are we in the right hotel?" Eddie whispered to me. I could see the worry tighten his features.

"Of course," I said sharply. "Why do you keep asking me these dumb questions? I'm not an idiot, you know. Why do you keep asking, is this the right room? Is this the right hotel?"

"Because nothing makes sense," he muttered.

I started to reply, but the clerk returned to the desk. "May I ask your room number?" he demanded, scratching his ear again.

"Six twenty-six," I told him.

He punched several keys on his computer keyboard, then squinted at the green monitor. "I'm sorry. That room is vacant," he said.

"What?" I cried.

The clerk studied me, narrowing his eyes. "There is no one in room 626 at the present," he repeated.

"But *we* are!" Eddie cried.

The clerk forced a smile to his face. He raised both hands, as if to say, "Let's all remain calm."

"We will find your parents," he told us, leaving the smile frozen on his face. He punched a few computer keys. "Now, what is your last name?"

I opened my mouth to answer. But no answer came to my mind.

I glanced at Eddie. His face was knitted in concentration.

"What is your last name, kids?" the clerk repeated. "If your parents are in the hotel, I'm sure we can track them down for you. But I need to know your last name."

I stared blankly at him.

I had a strange, tingly feeling that started at the back of my neck and ran all the way down my body. I suddenly felt as if I couldn't breathe, as if my heart had stopped.

My last name. My last name . . .

Why couldn't I remember my last name?

I could feel my body start to shake. Tears brimmed in my eyes.

This was so upsetting!

My name is Sue, I told myself. *Sue . . . Sue . . . what?*

Shaking, tears running down my cheeks, I grabbed Eddie by the shoulders. "Eddie," I demanded, "what's our last name?"

"I — I don't know!" he sobbed.

"Oh, Eddie!" I pulled my brother close and hugged him. "What's wrong with us? What's *wrong* with us?"

15

"We have to stay calm," I told my brother. "If we take a deep breath and just relax, I'm sure we'll be able to remember."

"I guess you're right," Eddie replied uncertainly. He stared straight ahead. He was gritting his teeth, trying hard not to cry.

It was a few minutes later. The desk clerk had suggested that we go to the hotel restaurant. He promised he'd try to find our parents while we ate.

That suggestion was fine with Eddie and me. We were both starving!

We sat at a small table in the back of the restaurant. I gazed around the big, elegant room. Crystal chandeliers cast sparkling light over the well-dressed diners. On a small balcony overlooking the room, a string quartet played classical music.

Eddie tapped his hands nervously on the white

tablecloth. I kept picking up the heavy silverware and twirling it in my hand.

The tables all around us were filled with laughing, happy people. Three children at the next table, very dressed up, were singing a song in French to their smiling parents.

Eddie leaned over the table and whispered to me. "How are we going to pay for the food? Our money isn't any good."

"We can charge it to the room," I replied. "When we figure out what room we're in." Eddie nodded and slouched back in his high-backed chair.

A waiter in a black tuxedo appeared beside the table. He smiled at Eddie and me. "Welcome to the Barclay," he said. "And what may I bring you this evening?"

"Could we see a menu?" I asked.

"There is no menu right now," the waiter replied, without changing his smile. "We are still serving tea."

"Only tea?" Eddie cried. "No food?"

The waiter chuckled. "Our high tea includes sandwiches, scones, croissants, and an assortment of pastries."

"Yes. We'll have that," I told him.

He gave a quick bow of his head, turned, and headed toward the kitchen.

"At least we'll get something to eat," I murmured.

Eddie didn't seem to hear me. He kept glancing at the doorway at the front of the restaurant. I know ho was looking for Mom and Dad.

"Why can't we remember our last name?" he asked glumly.

"I don't know," I confessed. "I'm very confused."

Every time I started to think about it, I felt dizzy. I kept telling myself I was just hungry. You'll remember after you've had something to eat, I kept repeating.

The waiter brought a tray of tiny sandwiches, cut into triangles. I recognized egg salad and tunafish. I didn't know what the others were.

But Eddie and I didn't care. We started devouring the sandwiches as soon as the waiter set them down.

We drank two cups of tea. Then our next tray arrived with scones and croissants. We loaded them up with butter and strawberry jam, and gobbled them down hungrily.

"Maybe if we tell the man at the front desk what Mom and Dad look like, he can help us find them," Eddie suggested. He grabbed the last croissant before I could get it.

"Good idea," I said.

Then I let out a silent gasp. I had the dizzy feeling again.

"Eddie," I said, "I can't remember what Mom and Dad look like!"

65

He let the croissant fall from his hand. "I can't either," he murmured, lowering his head. "This is crazy, Sue!"

I shut my eyes. "Shhh. Just try to picture them," I urged. "Force away all other thoughts. Concentrate. Try to picture then."

"I — I can't!" Eddie stammered. I could hear the panic in his high-pitched voice. "Something is wrong, Sue. Something is very wrong with us."

I swallowed hard. I opened my eyes. I couldn't conjure up any kind of picture of my parents.

I tried thinking about Mom. Was she blond? Red-haired? Black-haired? Was she tall? Short? Thin? Fat?

I couldn't remember.

"Where do we live?" Eddie wailed. "Do we live in a house? I can't picture it, Sue. I can't picture it at all."

His voice cracked. I could see he was having trouble holding back the tears.

Panic choked my throat. I suddenly felt as if I couldn't breathe. I stared at Eddie and couldn't say a word.

What could I say?

My brain spun like a tornado. "We've lost our memory," I finally uttered. "At least, part of our memory."

"How?" Eddie demanded in a trembling voice. "How could that happen to *both* of us?"

I clasped my hands tightly in my lap. My hands

were as cold as ice. "At least we still remember *some* things," I said, trying not to despair completely.

"We still remember our first names," Eddie replied. "But not our last. And what else do we remember?"

"We remember our room number," I said. "Six twenty-six."

"But the desk clerk said we don't belong in that room!" Eddie cried.

"And we remember *why* we came to London," I continued. "Because Mom and Dad had these important meetings."

"But there *are* no meetings at the hotel!" Eddie exclaimed. "Our memories are wrong, Sue. They're all wrong!"

I insisted on figuring out what we *did* remember. I had the feeling if I could list what we *did* remember, we wouldn't feel so upset about what we had forgotten.

I knew it was a crazy idea. But I didn't know what else to do.

"I remember the tour we took today," I said. "I remember everywhere we went in London. I remember Mr. Starkes. I remember —"

"What about yesterday?" Eddie interrupted. "What did we do yesterday, Sue?"

I started to reply, but my breath caught in my throat.

I couldn't remember yesterday!

Or the day before. Or the day before that.

"Oh, Eddie," I moaned, raising my hands to my cheeks, "something is terribly wrong."

Eddie didn't seem to hear me. His eyes were locked on the front of the restaurant.

I followed his gaze — and saw the slender, blond-haired man step into the room.

The taxi driver.

We had forgotten all about him!

16

I jumped up. The napkin fell off my lap, onto my shoe. I kicked it away and reached down to tug Eddie's arm. "Come on — let's get out of here."

Eddie gazed up at me uncertainly, then back at the taxi driver. The taxi driver had stopped just past the entrance. His eyes were searching each table.

"Hurry," I whispered. "He hasn't seen us yet."

"But maybe we should just explain to him —" Eddie said.

"Huh? Explain what?" I shot back. "That we can't pay him because we lost our memory and don't know our name? I really don't think he'll buy that — do you?"

Eddie twisted his face in a frown. "Okay. How do we get out of here?" he demanded.

The front door was blocked by the taxi driver. But I spotted a glass door on the back wall near our table.

The door had a filmy, white curtain over it and a small sign that read: No Exit.

But I didn't care. Eddie and I had no choice. We *had* to leave — fast!

I grabbed the knob and pulled the door open. Eddie and I slipped through, then tugged the door shut behind us.

"I don't think he saw us," I whispered. "I think we're okay."

We turned away from the door and found ourselves in a long, dark hallway. This must be an area used by the hotel workers, I thought. The floor had no carpet. The walls were dirty, stained, and unpainted.

We turned a corner. I held out a hand to stop Eddie.

We listened hard for footsteps. Had the taxi driver seen us duck out? Was he coming after us?

I couldn't hear a thing over the pounding of my heart. "What a horrible day!" I wailed.

And then the day turned even more horrible.

The man in the black cape stepped out from around the corner. "Did you really think I wouldn't follow you?" he asked. "Did you really think you could escape from *me*?"

17

He moved forward quickly, his face hidden in the shadows.

Eddie and I were trapped, our backs pressed against the curtained, glass door.

As the caped man drew near, his features came into view. His eyes were dark and cold. His mouth was locked in a menacing snarl.

He raised his palm to Eddie. "Give them back," he demanded.

Eddie's eyes bulged in surprise. "Huh? Give *what* back?" he cried.

The caped man kept his palm in front of Eddie's face. "Give them back — now!" he bellowed. "Do not play games with me."

Eddie's expression slowly changed. He glanced at me, then turned back to the caped man. "If I give them back, will you let us go?"

I was totally confused. *Give what back?* What was Eddie talking about?

The caped man uttered a short, dry laugh. It

71

sounded more like a cough. "Do you dare to bargain with me?" he asked my brother.

"Eddie — what is he *talking* about?" I cried.

But Eddie didn't reply. He kept his eyes locked on the shadowy face of the caped man. "If I give them back, will you let us go?"

"Hand them back — now," the big man replied sharply, leaning menacingly over Eddie.

Eddie sighed. He reached into his pants pocket. And to my shock, he pulled out the three smooth, white stones.

My brother the pickpocket had struck again. "Eddie — when did you take those?" I demanded.

"In the sewer," Eddie replied. "When he grabbed me."

"But, why?" I asked.

Eddie shrugged. "I don't know. They seemed important to him. So I thought —"

"They *are* important!" the caped man bellowed. He grabbed the stones from Eddie's hand.

"Now will you let us go?" Eddie cried.

"Yes. We will go now," the man replied, concentrating on the stones.

"That's *not* what I said!" Eddie exclaimed. "Will you let us go?"

The man ignored him. He piled the stones one on top of the other in his palm. Then he chanted some words, words in a foreign language that I didn't recognize.

As soon as he chanted the words, the hallway

began to shimmer. The doors began to wiggle and bend, as if made of rubber. The floor buckled and swayed.

The caped man began to shimmer and bend, too.

The hallway throbbed with a blinding, white light.

I felt a sharp stab of pain — as if I had been hit hard in the stomach.

I couldn't breathe.

Everything went black.

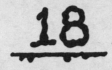

18

Flickering orange light broke the darkness.

I opened my eyes. Blinked several times. Took a deep breath.

The caped man was gone.

"Eddie — are you okay?" I asked in a quivering voice.

"I — I think so," he stammered.

I gazed down the long hall, startled to find it lit by flickering candles. A candle was perched in a holder beside each door.

"Sue, how did we get in this hallway?" Eddie asked softly. "Where is the caped man?"

"I don't know," I replied. "I'm as confused as you are."

We stepped into the flickering light. "This has to be the old section of the hotel," I guessed. "They must want it to look old-fashioned."

We walked past door after door. The long, narrow hallway was silent except for the thud of our

74

shoes on the hardwood floor. The doors were all closed. No other people in sight.

The flickering candlelight, the dark doorways, the eerie silence — all gave me a cold, tingly feeling. My entire body trembled.

We kept walking through the dim, orangey light.

"I — I want to go back to the room," Eddie stammered as we turned another corner. "Maybe Mom and Dad have come back. Maybe they're waiting for us up there."

"Maybe," I replied doubtfully.

We entered another silent hallway, glowing eerily in darting, dancing candlelight. "There's got to be an elevator down here somewhere," I muttered.

But we passed only dark, closed doors.

Turning another corner, we nearly bumped into a group of people.

"Ohh!" I cried out, so startled to find others in these long, empty hallways.

I stared at them as they passed. They wore long robes, and their faces were hidden under dark hoods. I couldn't tell if they were men or women.

They moved silently, making no sound at all. They paid no attention to Eddie or me.

"Uh . . . can you tell us where the elevator is?" Eddie called after them.

They didn't turn back, didn't reply.

"Sirs?" Eddie called, chasing after them. "Please! Have you seen the elevator?"

One of them turned back toward Eddie. The others continued moving silently down the hallway, their long robes swishing softly.

I stepped up beside my brother and the robed figure. I could see the face under the hood. An old man with bushy white eyebrows.

He peered out at Eddie, then at me. His eyes were dark and wet. His expression was sorrowful.

"I smell evil around you," he croaked in a dry whisper.

"What?" I cried. "My brother and I —"

"Do not leave the abbey," the old man instructed. "I smell evil around you. Your time is near. So near. So very near . . ."

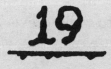

19

"What abbey?" I demanded. "Why are you saying that?"

The old man didn't reply. The candlelight glowed in his watery eyes. He nodded his head solemnly under the heavy hood. Then he turned away from us and glided silently after the others, the hem of his robe sweeping along the bare floor.

"What did he mean?" Eddie demanded when the hooded man had vanished around a corner. "Why did he try to frighten us?"

I shook my head. "It had to be some kind of a joke," I replied. "They're probably on their way to a party or something."

Eddie frowned thoughtfully. "They were creepy, Sue. They didn't look like they were in a party mood to me."

I sighed. "Let's find the elevator and get up to the room. I don't like this old part of the hotel. It's just too dark and scary."

"Hey, I'm the one who gets scared," Eddie said,

following me down the hall. "You're supposed to be the brave one — remember?"

We wandered down one long, candlelit hallway after another, feeling more and more lost. We couldn't find an elevator or stairs or any kind of exit.

"Are we going to walk forever?" Eddie whined. "There *has* to be a way out of here — doesn't there?"

"Let's go back," I suggested. "The taxi driver is probably gone by now. Let's go back the way we came, and go out through the restaurant."

Eddie pushed his dark hair back off his forehead. "Good idea," he muttered.

We turned and started the long walk back. It was easy to keep in the right direction. We followed the hallways and made left turns instead of rights.

We walked quickly without speaking.

As we walked, I tried to remember our last name. Tried to remember Mom and Dad. Tried to picture their faces.

Tried to remember *something* about them.

Losing your memory is so terrifying. Much more frightening than being chased by someone.

That's because the problem is inside you. Inside your own mind.

You can't run away from it. You can't hide from it. And you can't solve it.

You just feel so helpless.

My only hope was that Mom and Dad would be waiting in the room. And that they could explain to Eddie and me what had happened to our memories.

"Oh, no!" Eddie cried, startling me from my thoughts.

We had reached the end of the final hallway. The hotel restaurant should be on the other side of the curtained glass door.

But there was no door.

No door back to the restaurant. No door at all.

Eddie and I were staring at a solid wall.

20

"No!" Eddie wailed. "Let us out! Let us out of here!" He pounded furiously on the wall with his fist.

I tugged him away. "This must be the wrong hallway," I told him. "We made a wrong turn."

"No!" he protested. "It's the right hallway! I know it is!"

"Then where is the restaurant?" I replied. "They didn't seal it up while we were walking the halls just now."

He stared up at me, his chin trembling, his dark eyes frightened. "Can't we go outside and walk around to the front?" he asked wearily.

"We could," I replied thoughtfully. "If we could find a door that led to the outside. But so far —"

I stopped when I heard voices.

I turned and saw a narrow hallway leading off to our right. The voices seemed to be floating through this hall I hadn't noticed before. Voices and laughter.

"That must be the restaurant down there," I told Eddie. "See? We just had one more turn to make. We'll be out of here in a few seconds."

His face brightened a little.

The voices and laughter grew louder as we made our way down the narrow corridor. Bright yellow light shone out from an open doorway at the end.

As we stepped into the doorway, we both cried out in surprise.

This was not the hotel restaurant we had our tea in.

I grabbed Eddie's arm as I stared in shock around the enormous room. Two blazing fireplaces provided the only light. People in strange costumes sat on low benches around long, wooden tables.

A whole deer or an elk was turning on a spit, roasting over a fire in the center of the floor.

The tables were piled high with food — meats, whole cabbages, green vegetables, fruits, whole potatoes, and foods I didn't recognize.

I didn't see any plates or serving platters. The food was just strewn over the long tables. People reached in and pulled out what they wanted.

They ate noisily, talking loudly, laughing and singing, taking long drinks from metal wine cups, slapping the cups on the tabletop and toasting each other merrily.

"They're all eating with their *hands*!" Eddie exclaimed.

He was right. I didn't see any silverware at the tables.

Two chickens, squawking loudly, fluttered across the floor, chased by a large brown dog. A woman had two babies in her lap. She ignored them while she chewed on a large hunk of meat.

"It's a costume party," I whispered to Eddie. We hadn't the nerve to move from the doorway. "This must be where those guys in the hoods were going."

I gazed in amazement at the colorful costumes in the room. Long robes, loose-fitting pajama-type outfits of blue and green, leather vests worn over black tights. A lot of men and women wore animal furs around their shoulders — despite the blazing heat from the fireplaces.

In one corner, a man appeared to be wearing an entire bearskin. He stood beside a giant wooden barrel, working a spigot, filling metal cups with a thick, brown liquid that oozed from the barrel.

Two children in rags played tag under one of the long tables. Another child, dressed in green tights, chased after one of the squawking chickens.

"What a party!" Eddie whispered. "Who *are* these people?"

I shrugged. "I don't know. I can't understand what they're saying too well. Can you?"

Eddie shook his head. "Their accents are too weird."

"But maybe someone in here can tell us how to get outside," I suggested.

"Let's try," Eddie pleaded.

I led the way into the room. Even though I was walking slowly, timidly, I nearly tripped over a sleeping hound dog.

Eddie followed close behind as I made my way up to one of the men turning the roasting deer on the spit. He wore only knee breeches of some rough brown cloth. His forehead and the top of his body glistened with sweat.

"Excuse me, sir," I said.

He glanced up at me and his eyes bulged wide in surprise.

"Excuse me," I repeated. "Can you tell us how to get out of the hotel?"

He stared at me without replying, stared as if he had never seen a twelve-year-old girl in jeans and a T-shirt before.

Two little girls, wearing gray dresses down to the floor, walked up to Eddie and me, staring up at us with the same shocked expression as the man. Their streaky blond hair fell wild and tangled behind their backs. It looked as if it had never been brushed in their lives!

They pointed at us and giggled.

And I suddenly realized that the entire room had grown silent.

As if someone had turned a knob and clicked off the sound.

My heart started to pound. The strong smell of the roasting deer choked my nostrils.

I turned to find everyone in the room gaping in open-mouthed wonder. Staring in silence at Eddie and me.

"I — I'm sorry to interrupt the party," I stammered in a tiny, frightened voice.

I let out a cry of surprise as they all climbed noisily to their feet. Food toppled off the table. One of the long benches clattered to the floor.

More children pointed and giggled.

Even the chickens seemed to stop clucking and strutting.

And then an enormous red-faced man in a long white gown raised his hand and pointed at Eddie and me. *"It's THEM!"* he bellowed. *"It's THEM!"*

21

"Do they *know* us?" Eddie whispered to me.

We stared back at them. Everyone seemed to freeze in place. The man stopped turning the deer on the spit. The only sound in the huge dining hall was the crackle of the fires in the twin fireplaces.

The man in the white gown slowly lowered his hand. His face darkened to a bright scarlet as he gaped at us in amazement.

"We just want to find the way out," I said. My voice sounded tiny and shrill.

No one moved. No one replied.

I took a deep breath and tried one more time. "Can anyone help us?"

Silence.

Who are these strange people? I wondered. *Why are they staring at us like that? Why won't they answer us?*

Eddie and I took a step back as they began to move toward us. Some of them were whispering excitedly, muttering to each other, gesturing with their hands.

"Eddie — we'd better get out of here!" I whispered.

I couldn't hear what they were saying. But I didn't like the excited expressions on their faces.

And I didn't like the way they were moving along the wall, moving to get behind us, to surround us.

"Eddie — run!" I screamed.

Angry cries rang out as we both spun around and hurtled toward the open doorway. Dogs barked. Children started to cry.

We darted back into the dark hallway and kept running.

I could still feel the heat of the fire on my face as we ran, still smell the tangy aroma of the roasting deer.

Their excited, angry cries followed us through the long hall. Gasping for breath, I glanced back, expecting to see them chasing after us.

But the hall was empty.

We turned a corner and kept going. Candles flickered on both sides of us. The floorboards groaned under our shoes.

The eerie, dim light. The voices far behind us. The endless tunnel of a hallway. All made me feel as if I were running through a dream.

We turned another corner and kept running.

The misty candlelight blurred as I ran. I'm floating through a dark orange cloud, I thought.

Do these empty, candlelit halls ever end?

Eddie and I both cried out happily as a door appeared in front of us.

A door we had never seen before.

It *has* to lead to the outside! I told myself.

We raced to the door. We didn't slow down as we reached it.

I stuck out both hands. Pushed hard.

The door flew open.

And we stepped out into bright sunlight.

Outside! We had escaped from the dark maze of the hotel corridors!

It took a few seconds for the harsh white glare to fade from my eyes.

I blinked several times. Then I gazed up and down the street.

"Oh, no!" I wailed, grabbing my brother's arm. "No! Eddie — what has *happened?*"

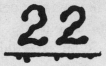

22

"It — it's daytime!" Eddie stammered.

But the bright sunlight wasn't the only shock.

Everything had changed.

I felt as if I were watching a movie, and the scene had changed. And suddenly it was the next day — or the next week — and I was seeing an entirely different place.

I knew that only a few seconds had passed since Eddie and I had burst out of the hotel. But in that time, *everything* had changed.

We huddled close together and stared in one direction and then the next. We saw no cars. No buses. The street had vanished, replaced by a lumpy dirt road.

The tall buildings had disappeared, too. The road was dotted with small, white cottages with flat roofs and low, wooden shacks built without doors or windows.

A tall mound of straw stood beside the nearest cottage. Chickens clucked and strutted across the road or stood in front of cottages pecking in the dirt. A brown cow poked its head out from behind the mound of straw.

"What's going on?" Eddie asked. "Where are we?"

"It's like we stepped back in time," I said in a hushed voice. "Eddie — look at the people."

Two men walked by carrying lines of slender, silvery fish. The men had thick beards and wild, unbrushed hair. They wore loose-fitting gray smocks that dragged along the ground.

Two women in long, brown dresses were on their knees, pulling up root-type vegetables with their hands. A man leading a scrawny horse, its bones sticking out at its rib cage, stopped to say something to the two women.

"They look a lot like the people in the hotel," I told Eddie.

Thinking about the hotel made me turn around. "Oh, no!" I grabbed Eddie and made him turn around.

The hotel was gone.

In its place stood a long, low building built of brown stone. It appeared to be some sort of inn or meeting hall.

"I don't understand this," Eddie moaned. In the bright sunlight, he looked very pale. He scratched his dark brown hair. "Sue, we've got to get back to the hotel. I — I'm very mixed up."

"Me, too," I confessed.

I took a few steps along the dirt road. It must have rained recently. The road was soft and muddy.

I could hear cows mooing nearby.

This is downtown London! I told myself. How can I hear cows in downtown London? Where are all the tall buildings? The cars and taxis and double-decker buses?

I heard someone whistling. A blond-haired boy, dressed in an outfit made of black and brown rags, appeared from behind the long building. He carried a bundle of sticks in his arms.

He seemed about my age. My shoes sank into the mud as I hurried across the road to him. "Hey —!" I called. "Hi!"

He peered over the bundle of sticks at me. His blue eyes widened in surprise. His hair was long and unbrushed. It fluttered over his shoulders in the breeze. "Good day to you, miss," he said. His accent was so strange, I could barely understand him.

"Good day," I replied uncertainly.

"Are ye a traveler?" the boy asked, shifting the bundle onto his shoulder.

"Yes," I replied. "But my brother and I are lost. We can't find our hotel."

He narrowed his blue eyes at me. He appeared to be thinking hard.

"Our hotel," I repeated. "Can you tell us where it is? The Barclay?"

"Barclay?" he repeated the word. "Hotel?"

"Yes," I said. I waited for him to reply. But he just stared back at me, squinting his blue eyes and frowning.

"I do not know those foreign words," he said finally.

"Hotel?" I cried impatiently. "You know. A place where travelers stay?"

"Many stay at the abbey," he replied. He pointed to the long, low building behind us.

"No. I mean —" I started. I could see that he didn't understand me at all.

"I must be getting the wood along home," the boy said. He nodded good-bye, lowered the bundle from his shoulder, and headed down the road.

"Eddie, that boy —" I said. "He doesn't know what a hotel is! Do you believe —?"

I turned back. "Eddie?"

Eddie was gone.

23

"Eddie? Eddie?"

My voice grew higher and more frightened as I called his name.

Where did he go?

"Hey — Eddie!" I shouted.

The two women glanced up from their vegetable picking.

"Did you see where my brother went?" I called to them.

They shook their heads and returned to their work.

"Oh!" I had to jump out of the road as a cart, pulled by a groaning, grunting ox, came barreling past. The driver, a fat, bare-chested man, his pouchy skin darkened by the sun, slapped the ropes that served as reins. He bellowed at the ox to move faster.

As the wagon rolled past, its wooden wheels sank into the mud, leaving deep ridges in the road.

Chickens clucked and scurried out of the way. The two women didn't even glance up.

I made my way to the entrance of the abbey. "Eddie? Are you back here?"

I pulled open the door and peered inside. The long candlelit hall stretched before me. I could see men in hooded robes gathered at a doorway.

We just came from there, I told myself as I closed the door. Eddie wouldn't go back inside.

So where was he?

How could he run off and leave me here? How could he just disappear like that?

I called his name a few more times. Then my throat tightened up. My mouth felt dry as cotton. "Eddie?" I called weakly.

My legs began to tremble as I walked to the side of the first cottage. *Don't panic, Sue,* I told myself. You'll find him. Just don't panic.

Too late.

I was really scared.

Eddie wouldn't suddenly wander off and go exploring without me. He was too scared.

So where was he?

I peered into the open doorway of the cottage. A sour smell floated out from inside. I could see a crude wooden table and a couple of wooden stools. No one in there.

I made my way behind the cottage. A grassy pasture stretched up a gently sloping hill. Four or five cows stood halfway up the hill, their heads lowered as they chewed the grass.

I cupped my hands around my mouth and called to my brother.

My only reply was the soft mooing of a cow.

With a worried sigh, I turned around and made my way back to the road. I guess I'll have to search every cottage, I decided. Eddie couldn't have gone very far.

I had only taken a few steps toward the next cottage when a shadow slid over the road.

Startled, I raised my eyes — and stared at the dark figure blocking my path.

His black cape fluttered behind him in the wind. He wore a new black hat, and his pale, pale face poked out from its dark brim.

24

I stepped back, out of his shadow. I raised my hands to my cheeks and stared at him in horrified silence.

"I said it was time for us to go," he said softly, moving closer.

"Wh-where is Eddie?" I managed to choke out. "Do you know where Eddie is?"

A thin-lipped smile crossed his pale face. "Eddie?" He snickered. For some reason, my question seemed to amuse him. "Do not worry about *Eddie*," he replied with a sneer.

He took another step forward. His shadow fell over me again.

It made me shiver.

Glancing around, I saw that the two women picking vegetables had disappeared into their cottages. Everyone had disappeared. The road stood empty except for some chickens and a hound dog, asleep on its side in front of the straw pile.

"I — I don't understand," I stammered. "Who are you? Why are you chasing us? Where *are* we?"

My frantic questions only made him chuckle. "You know me," he replied softly.

"No!" I protested. "I don't know you! What is happening?"

"Your questions cannot delay your fate," he replied.

I stared hard at him, trying to study his face, searching for answers. But he lowered the brim of the black hat, hiding his eyes from view.

"You've made a mistake!" I cried. "You've got the wrong girl! I don't know you! I don't know anything!"

His smile faded. He shook his head. "Come with me now," he said firmly.

"No!" I shrieked. "Not until you tell me who you are! Not until you tell me where my brother is."

Brushing his heavy cape back, he took another step toward me. His boots sank heavily into the mud as he strode forward.

"I won't come with you!" I screamed. My hands were still pressed hard against my cheeks. My legs were shaking so much, I nearly sank to the ground.

I glanced around, getting ready to run.

Would my trembling legs carry me?

"Do not think of running away," he said, as if reading my mind.

"But — but —" I sputtered.

"You will come with me now. It is time," he said.

He strode forward quickly, raised his gloved hands, and grabbed me by both shoulders.

I had no time to struggle. No time to try to break free.

The ground started to rumble.

I heard a groaning sound. A heavy slapping sound.

Another oxcart bounced around the corner. I saw the driver slap the ox with a long rope.

The cart moved so fast. A blur of groaning animal and grinding wheels.

The black-caped man released his grasp and leaped back as the cart rolled at us.

I saw his black hat fly off. Saw him stumble in the deep rut in the mud at the side of the road. Saw him stagger back off-balance.

It was all the time I needed. I wheeled around and started to run. I bent low as I ran, hiding beside the grunting, straining ox. Then I turned sharply and dived between two small cottages.

I caught a glimpse of the black-caped man as I darted past the cottages. He was bending to pick up his hat. His bald head shone like an egg in the sunlight. He had no hair at all.

I was panting rapidly. My chest ached, and the blood throbbed at my temples.

Keeping low, I ran along the backs of the cottages. The green pasture stretched to my left. Nowhere to hide there.

The cottages grew closer together. I heard crying children. A woman was roasting some kind of blood-red sausage over a fire. She called out to me as I ran past. But I didn't slow down to reply.

Two scrawny black hounds came yapping after me, snapping at my legs. "Shoo!" I cried. "Shoo! Go home!"

Glancing back, I could see the tall, dark figure gliding easily over the grass, his cape sweeping up behind him.

He's catching up, I realized.

I have to find a hiding place, I told myself. Now!

I ducked between two small shacks — and nearly ran into a large, red-haired woman carrying a baby. The baby was swaddled in a heavy, gray blanket. Startled, the woman squeezed the baby to her chest.

"You've got to hide me!" I cried breathlessly.

"Go away from here!" the woman replied. She seemed more frightened than unfriendly.

"Please!" I begged. "He's chasing me!" I pointed through the space between the cottages.

98

We could both see the black-caped man running closer.

"Please! Don't let him catch me!" I pleaded. "Hide me! Hide me!"

The woman had her eyes on the black-caped man. She turned to me and shrugged her broad shoulders. "I cannot," she said.

25

I let out a long sigh, a sigh of defeat. I knew I couldn't run any further.

I knew the caped man would capture me easily.

The woman pressed the baby against the front of her black dress and turned to watch the man run toward us.

"I — I'll *pay* you!" I blurted out.

I suddenly remembered the coins in my pocket. The coins the taxi driver refused to take.

Would the woman take them now?

I shoved my hand into my pocket and pulled out the coins. "Here!" I cried. "Take them! Take them all! Just hide me — please!"

I jammed the coins into the woman's free hand.

As she raised her hand to examine them, her eyes bulged and her mouth dropped open.

She isn't going to take them, either, I thought. She's going to throw them back at me as the taxi driver did.

But I was wrong.

"Gold sovereigns!" she exclaimed in a hushed voice. "Gold sovereigns. I saw one once when I was a little lass."

"Will you take them? Will you hide me?" I pleaded.

She dropped the coins into her dress. Then she shoved me through the open doorway of her little cottage.

It smelled of fish inside. I saw three cots on the floor beside a bare hearth.

"Quick — into the kindling basket," the woman instructed. "It's empty." She pushed me again, toward a large straw box with a lid.

My heart pounding, I pushed up the lid and scrambled inside. The lid dropped back down, covering me in darkness.

On my hands and knees, I crouched on the rough straw bottom of the box. I struggled to stop panting, to stop my heart from thudding in my chest.

The woman had taken the coins gladly, I realized. She didn't think they were play money, as the taxi driver had said.

The coins are very old, I decided.

And then a chill ran down my trembling body. I suddenly knew why everything looked so different — so old. We really have gone back in time, I told myself.

We are back in London hundreds of years ago.

The caped man brought us back here with those white stones. He thinks I am someone else. He has been chasing me because he has mistaken me for someone else.

How do I make him see the truth? I wondered.

And how do I get out of the past, back to my real time?

I forced the questions from my mind — and listened.

I could hear voices outside the cottage. The woman's voice. And then the booming, deep voice of the black-caped man.

I held my breath so I could hear their words over the loud beating of my heart.

"She is right in here, sire," the woman said. I heard footsteps. And then their voices became louder. Closer. They were standing beside my basket.

"Where is she?" the caped man demanded.

"I put her in this box for you, sire," the woman replied. "She's all wrapped up for you. Ready for you to take her away."

26

My heart jumped to my throat. In the blackness of the box, I suddenly saw red.

That woman took my money, I thought angrily. And then she gave away my hiding place.

How could she do that to me?

I was still crouched on my hands and knees. So angry. So terrified. My entire body went numb, and I felt as if I would crumple to the basket floor in a heap.

Taking a deep breath, I twisted around and tried to push open the straw lid.

I let out a disappointed groan when it didn't budge.

Was it clasped shut? Or was the caped man holding it down?

It didn't matter. I was helpless. Trapped. I was his prisoner now.

The basket suddenly moved, knocking me against its side. I could feel it sliding over the floor of the cottage.

"Hey —!" I cried out. But my voice was muffled in the tiny box. I lowered myself to the rough straw floor, my heart pounding. "Let me out!"

The basket bounced again. Then I felt it slide some more.

"Lass! You — lass!" I lifted my head as I heard the woman whispering in to me.

"I am so sorry," she said. "I hope you will find it in your heart to forgive me. But I dare not go against the Lord High Executioner."

"What?" I cried. "What did you say?"

The basket slid faster. Bumped hard. Bumped again.

"What did you say?" I repeated frantically.

Silence now.

I did not hear her voice again.

A moment later, I heard the whinny of horses. I was tossed against one side, then the other, as the basket was lifted up.

Soon after, the basket began to bounce and shake. And I heard the steady *clip-clop* of horses' hooves.

A helpless prisoner inside the straw basket, I knew I was on some kind of carriage or horse cart.

The Lord High Executioner?

Is that what the woman had said?

The shadowy man in the black cape and black hat — he is the Lord High Executioner?

Inside my tiny, dark prison, I began to shudder. I could not stop the chills that rolled down my back until my entire body felt cold and numb and tingly.

The Lord High Executioner.

The words kept repeating and repeating in my mind. Like a terrifying chant.

The Lord High Executioner.

And then I asked myself: *What does he want with me?*

27

The wagon stopped with a jolt. Then, a minute or so later, started up again.

Bouncing around inside the basket, I lost all track of time.

Where is he taking me? I wondered. What does he plan to do?

And: *Why me?*

My head hit the front of the basket as we jolted to another stop. I shivered. My body was drenched in a cold sweat.

The air in the box had become sour. I began gasping for fresh air.

I let out a cry as the lid suddenly flew open. The harsh sunlight made me shield my eyes.

"Remove her!" I heard the booming voice of the Executioner.

Strong arms grabbed me roughly and tugged me from the straw box. As my eyes adjusted to the light, I saw that I was being lifted by two gray-uniformed soldiers.

They set me on my feet. But my legs gave way, and I crumpled to the dirt.

"Stand her up," the Executioner ordered. I gazed up into the sun at him. His face was hidden once again in the shadow of his dark hat.

The soldiers bent to pick me up. Both of my legs had fallen asleep. My back ached from being tossed and tumbled in the cramped box.

"Let me go!" I managed to cry. "Why are you doing this?"

The Executioner didn't reply.

The soldiers held on to me until I could stand on my own.

"You've made a terrible mistake!" I told him, my voice trembling with anger, with fear. "I don't know why I am here or how I got here! But I am the wrong girl! I am not who you think I am!"

Again, he did not reply. He gave a signal with one hand, and the guards took my arms and turned me around.

And as I turned away from the Executioner, away from the sun, the dark castle rose in front of me. I saw the wall, the courtyard, the dark, slender towers looming up over the stone castle.

The Terror Tower!

He had brought me to the Terror Tower.

This is where Eddie and I had seen him for the first time. This is where the Executioner had first chased after us.

In the twentieth century. In my time. In the

time where I belonged. Hundreds of years in the future.

Somehow Eddie and I had been dragged back into the past, to a time where we didn't belong. And now Eddie was lost. And I was being led to the Terror Tower.

The Executioner led the way. The soldiers gripped my arms firmly, pulling me through the courtyard toward the castle entrance.

The courtyard was jammed with silent, grim-looking people. Dressed in rags and tattered, stained gowns, they stared at me as I was dragged past.

Some of them stood hunched like scarecrows, their eyes vacant, their faces blank, as if their minds were somewhere else. Some sat and wept, or stared at the sky.

A bare-chested old man sat under a tree frantically scratching his greasy tangles of white hair with both hands. A young man pressed a filthy rag against a deep cut in his dirt-caked foot.

Babies cried and wailed. Men and women sat in the dirt, moaning and muttering to themselves.

These sad, filthy people were all prisoners, I realized. I remembered our tour guide, Mr. Starkes, telling us that the castle had first been a fort, then a prison.

I shook my head sadly, wishing I were back on the tour. In the future, in the time where I belonged.

I didn't have long to think about the prisoners. I was shoved into the darkness of the castle. Dragged up the twisting stone steps.

The air felt wet and cold as I climbed. A heavy chill seemed to rise up the stairs with me.

"Let me go!" I screamed. "Please — let me go!"

The soldiers shoved me against the stone wall when I tried to pull free.

I cried out helplessly and tried again to tug myself loose. But they were too big, too strong.

The stone stairs curved round and around. We passed the cell on the narrow landing. Glancing toward it, I saw that it was jammed with prisoners. They stood in silence against the bars, their faces yellow and expressionless. Many of them didn't even look up as I passed.

Up the steep, slippery stairs.

Up to the dark door at the top of the tower.

"No — please!" I begged. "This is all wrong! All wrong!"

But they slid the heavy metal bolt on the door and pulled the door open.

A hard shove from behind sent me sprawling into the tiny tower room. I stumbled to the floor, landing on my elbows and knees.

I heard the heavy door slam behind me. Then I heard the bolt sliding back into place.

Locked in.

I was locked in the tiny cell at the top of the Terror Tower.

"Sue!" A familiar voice called my name.

I raised myself to my knees. Glanced up. "Eddie!" I cried happily. "Eddie — how did you get here?"

My little brother had been sitting on the floor against the wall. Now he scrambled over to me and helped me to my feet. "Are you okay?" he asked.

I nodded. "Are *you* okay?"

"I guess," he replied. He had a long dirt smear down one side of his face. His dark hair was matted wetly against his forehead. His eyes were red-rimmed and frightened.

"The caped man grabbed me," Eddie said. "Back in the town. In the street. You know. When that oxcart came by."

I nodded. "I turned around, and you were gone."

"I tried to call to you," Eddie replied. "But the caped man covered my mouth. He handed me to his soldiers. And they pulled me behind one of the cottages."

"This is so awful!" I cried, struggling to hold my tears back.

"One of the soldiers lifted me onto his horse," Eddie said. "I tried to squirm away. But I couldn't. He brought me to the castle and dragged me up to the Tower."

"The caped man — he's the Lord High Executioner," I told my brother. "That's what I heard a woman call him."

The words made my brother gasp. His dark eyes locked onto mine. "Executioner?"

I nodded grimly.

"But why does he want *us*?" Eddie demanded. "Why has he been chasing *us*? Why are we locked up in this horrible tower?"

A sob escaped my throat. "I — I don't know," I stammered.

I started to say something else — but stopped when I heard noises outside the door.

Eddie and I huddled together in the center of the room.

I heard the bolt slide open.

The door slowly began to open.

Someone was coming for us.

28

A white-haired man stepped into the room. His hair was wild and long, and fell in thick tangles behind his shoulders. He had a short white beard that ended in a sharp point.

He wore a purple robe that flowed down to the floor. His eyes were as purple as his robe. They squinted first at Eddie, then lingered on me.

"You have returned," he said solemnly. His voice was smooth and low. His purple eyes suddenly revealed sadness.

"Who are you?" I cried. "Why have you locked us in this tower?"

"Let us out!" Eddie demanded shrilly. "Let us out of here — right now!"

The long purple robe swept over the floor as the white-haired man moved toward us. He shook his head sadly, but didn't reply.

The cries and moans of prisoners down below floated into the tower room through the tiny window above our heads. Gray evening light spilled over us.

"You do not remember me," the man said softly.

"Of course not!" Eddie cried. "We don't belong here!"

"You've made a bad mistake," I told him.

"You do not remember me," he repeated, rubbing his pointed beard with one hand. "But you will."

He seemed gentle. Kind. Not at all like the Executioner.

But as his strange purple eyes locked on mine, I felt a shiver of fear. This man was powerful, I realized. This man was dangerous.

"Just let us go!" Eddie pleaded again.

The man sighed. "I wish it were in my power to release you, Edward," he said softly. "I wish it were in my power to release you, too, Susannah."

"Wait a minute." I held up a hand to signal *stop*. "Just wait a minute. My name is Sue. Not Susannah."

The old man's hands disappeared into the deep pockets of his robe. "Perhaps I should introduce myself," he said. "My name is Morgred. I am the king's sorcerer."

"You do magic tricks?" Eddie blurted out.

"Tricks?" The old man seemed confused by Eddie's question.

"Did you order us locked up in here?" I asked him. "Did you have us brought back in time? Why? Why have you done this?"

"It isn't an easy story to tell, Susannah," Morgred replied. "You and Edward have to believe —"

"Stop calling me Susannah!" I shouted.

"I'm not Edward!" my brother insisted. "I'm Eddie. Everyone calls me Eddie."

The old man removed his hands from his robe pockets. He placed one hand on Eddie's shoulder, and one on mine.

"I had better start with the biggest surprise of all," he told us. "You are not Eddie and Sue. And you do not live in the twentieth century."

"Huh? What are you *saying*?" I cried.

"You really are Edward and Susannah," Morgred replied. "You are the Prince and Princess of York. And you have been ordered to the Tower by your uncle, the king."

29

"You're wrong!" Eddie cried. "We know who we are. You've made a big mistake!"

I suddenly felt cold all over. Morgred's words echoed in my ears. "You are not Eddie and Sue. You really are Edward and Susannah."

I took a step back, out from under his hand. I studied his face. Was he joking? Was he crazy?

His eyes revealed only sadness. His expression remained solemn, too solemn to be joking.

"I do not expect you to believe me," Morgred said, returning his hands to his robe pockets. "But my words are true. I cast a spell upon you. I tried to help you escape."

"Escape?" I cried. "You mean — escape from this tower?"

Morgred nodded. "I tried to help you escape your fate."

And as he said this, the voice of Mr. Starkes, the tour guide, returned to my ears. And I remembered the story he had told. I remembered the fate of Prince Edward and Princess Susannah.

The king's orders were to smother them.

Smothered with pillows.

"But we're not them!" I wailed. "You're just confused. Maybe Eddie and I look like them. Maybe we look a *lot* like them. But we're not the prince and princess. We're two kids from the twentieth century."

Morgred shook his head solemnly. "I cast a spell," he explained. "I erased your memories. You were locked in this tower. I wanted you to escape. First I whisked you away to the safety of the abbey, then I sent you as far into the future as I could."

"It's not true!" Eddie insisted, shrieking the words. "It's not true! Not true! I'm Eddie — not Edward. My name is Eddie!"

Morgred sighed again. "Just Eddie?" he asked, keeping his voice low and soft. "What is your full name, Eddie?"

"I — uh — well . . ." my brother stammered.

Eddie and I don't know our last name, I realized. And we don't know where we live.

"When I sent you far into the future, I gave you new memories," Morgred said. "I gave you new memories so you could survive in a new and distant time. But the memories were not complete."

"That's why we couldn't remember our parents!" I exclaimed to Eddie.

"But our parents —?" I started.

"Your parents, the rightful king and queen, are dead," Morgred told us. "Your uncle has named himself king. And he has ordered you to the Tower to get you out of the way."

"He — he's going to have us *murdered!*" I stammered.

Morgred nodded, shutting his eyes. "Yes. I am afraid he is. His men will be here soon. There is no way I can stop him now."

30

"I don't believe this," Eddie murmured. "I really don't."

But I could see the sadness in Morgred's purple eyes and hear it in his low, soft voice. The sorcerer was telling the truth.

The horror of the truth was sinking in. My brother and I weren't Eddie and Sue from the twentieth century. We lived in this dark and dangerous time. We were Edward and Susannah of York.

"I tried to send you as far from this Tower as possible," Morgred tried to explain again. "I sent you far into the future to start new lives. I wanted you to live there and never return. Never return to face doom in this castle."

"But what happened?" I demanded. "Why, then, are we back here, Morgred?"

"The Lord High Executioner was spying on me," Morgred explained, lowering his voice to a

118

whisper. "He must have known that I wanted to help you escape. And, so —"

He stopped and tilted his head toward the door. Was that a footstep? Was someone out there? All three of us listened.

Silence now.

Morgred continued his story in a whisper. "When I cast the spell that sent you into the future, the Executioner must have hidden nearby. I used three white stones to cast the spell. Later, he stole the stones and performed the spell himself. He sent himself to the future to bring you back. And as you both know, he caught you and dragged you back here."

Morgred took a step forward. He raised his hand and placed it on my forehead.

The hand felt cold at first. Then it grew warmer and warmer, until I pulled away from the blazing heat.

As I pulled back, my memory returned.

Once again, I became Princess Susannah of York. My true identity. I remembered my parents, the king and queen. And all my memories of growing up in the royal castle returned.

My brother glared angrily at Morgred. "What did you do to my sister?" he cried, backing up until he bumped into the stone wall.

Morgred placed his hand on my brother's forehead. And I watched my brother's expression change as his memory returned and he realized he really was the prince.

"How did you do it, Morgred?" Edward asked, pushing his dark brown hair off his forehead. "How did you send Susannah and me to the future? Can you perform the spell again?"

"Yes!" I cried. "Can you perform it once more? Can you send us to the future now — before the king's men come?"

Morgred shook his head sadly. "Alas, I cannot," he murmured. "I do not have the three stones. As I told you, they were stolen by the Lord High Executioner."

A smile slowly spread over my brother's face. He reached into his pocket. "Here they are!" Eddie announced. He winked at me. "I stole them back again when the Executioner captured me in town."

Edward handed the stones to Morgred. "Fastest hands in all of Britannia!" he declared.

Morgred did not smile. "It is a simple spell, actually," the wizard said. He raised the three stones into the air, and they began to glow.

"I pile the stones up one on top of the other," Morgred explained. "I wait for them to glow with a bright white heat. Then I pronounce the words *'Movarum, Lovaris, Movarus.'* I then call out the year to which the traveler is to be sent."

"That's the whole spell?" Edward asked, staring at the smooth, glowing stones in Morgred's hand.

Morgred nodded. "That is the spell, Prince Edward."

"Well, do it again! Please hurry!" I begged him.

His expression grew even sadder. "I cannot," he said, his voice breaking with emotion.

He returned the three stones to the pocket of his robe. Then he uttered a long, unhappy sigh. "It is my fondest wish to help you children," he whispered. "But if I help you to escape again, the king will torture me and put me to a painful death. And then I will not be able to use my magic to help all the people of Britain."

Tears brimmed in his purple eyes and ran down his wrinkled cheeks. He gazed unhappily at my brother and me. "I — I only hope that you enjoyed your brief time in the future," he said in a whisper.

I shuddered. "You — you really cannot help us?" I pleaded.

"I cannot," he replied, lowering his eyes to the floor.

"Even if we *ordered* you?" Edward asked.

"Even if you ordered me," Morgred repeated. With an emotional cry, he wrapped Edward in a hug. Then he turned and hugged me, too. "I am helpless," he whispered. "I beg your forgiveness. But I am helpless."

"How long do we have to live?" I asked in a tiny, trembling voice.

"Perhaps a few hours," Morgred replied, avoiding my eyes. He turned away. He could not bear to face us.

A heavy silence fell over the tiny room. The gray light filtered down from the window above our heads. The air suddenly felt cold and damp.

I couldn't stop shivering.

Edward startled me by leaning close and whispering in my ear. "Susannah, look!" he whispered excitedly. "The door. Morgred left the door open when he entered."

I turned to the door. Edward was right. The heavy wooden door stood nearly half open.

We still have a chance, I thought, my heart beginning to race. We still have a tiny chance.

"Edward — *run!*" I screamed.

31

I took a running step.

And froze in midair.

I turned to see Edward freeze, too, his arms outstretched, his legs bent in a running position.

I struggled to move. But I couldn't. I felt as if my body had turned to stone.

It took me a few seconds to realize that Morgred had cast a spell on us. Frozen stiffly in the center of the tiny room, I watched the sorcerer make his way to the door.

Halfway out, he turned back to us. "I'm so sorry," he said in a trembling voice. "But I cannot allow you to escape. Please understand. I did my best. I really did. But now I am helpless. Truly helpless."

Tears rolled down his cheeks, into his white beard. He gave us one last sad glance. Then the door slammed hard behind him.

As soon as the door was bolted from the outside, the spell wore off. Edward and I could move again.

I sank to the floor. I suddenly felt weak. Weary.

Edward stood tensely beside me, his eyes on the door.

"What are we going to do?" I asked my brother. "Poor Morgred. He tried to help us. He wanted to help us again. But he couldn't. If only —"

I stopped talking when I heard the heavy footsteps outside the door.

At first, I thought it was Morgred returning.

But then I heard hushed voices. The sounds of more than one man.

Right outside the door now.

And I recognized the booming voice of one of them. The Lord High Executioner.

I climbed tensely to my feet and turned to Edward. "They've come for us," I whispered.

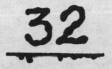

32

To my surprise, Edward's face remained calm.

He raised his hand. He had something hidden in his closed fist.

As he opened his fist, I recognized the three stones. Morgred's smooth, white stones.

They immediately began to glow.

"Edward — again?" I cried.

A smile crossed his lips. His dark eyes lit up excitedly. "I lifted them from Morgred's robe when he hugged me."

"Do you remember the spell?" I demanded.

Edward's smile faded. "I — I think so."

I could hear the Executioner outside the door. The heavy treading of boots on the stone stairs.

"Edward — please hurry!" I urged.

I heard the bolt slide outside the door.

I heard the heavy wooden door begin to slide open.

Edward struggled to stack the glowing stones

one on top of the other. The one on top kept slipping off.

Finally, he held all three in a small tower in his palm.

The door slid open a few inches more.

Edward held the glowing stones high. And called out the words, *"Movarum, Lovaris, Movarus!"*

The glowing stones exploded in a flash of white light.

The light faded quickly.

I glanced around.

"Oh, Edward!" I wailed in disappointment. "It didn't work! We're still in the Tower!"

Before my stunned brother could reply, the door swung all the way open.

33

And there they stood. A tour group.

I didn't recognize the tour leader. She was a young woman, dressed in layers of red and yellow T-shirts, and a short skirt over black tights.

I grinned at Edward. I felt so happy, I didn't think I would ever stop grinning!

"You did it, Edward!" I cried. "You did it! Your spell *did* work!"

"Call me Eddie," he replied, laughing gleefully. "Call me Eddie, okay, *Sue*?"

The spell had worked perfectly. We were back in the twentieth century. Back in the Tower — as tourists!

"This tiny Tower room is where Prince Edward and Princess Susannah of York were held as prisoners," the tour guide announced. "They were held here and sentenced to death. But they were never executed."

"They didn't die up here?" I asked the tour guide. "What happened?"

The tour guide shrugged. She chewed her gum harder. "No one knows. On the night they were to be murdered, the prince and princess vanished. Disappeared into thin air. It is a mystery that will never be solved."

Members of the tour group mumbled to each other, gazing around the small room.

"Look at the thick, stone walls," the tour guide continued, chewing her gum as she talked. "Look at the barred window so high above. How did they escape? We will never know."

"I guess *we* know the answer to the mystery," someone whispered behind me.

Eddie and I turned to see Morgred grinning at us. He winked. I saw that he was wearing a purple sports jacket and dark gray trousers.

"Thanks for bringing me along," he said happily.

"We had to bring you, Morgred," Eddie replied. "We need a parent."

Morgred raised a finger to his mouth. "Hush! Don't call me Morgred. I'm Mr. Morgan now. Okay?"

"Okay," I said. "And I guess I'm Sue Morgan. And this is Eddie Morgan." I slapped my brother on the back.

The tour group started out of the Tower room, and we followed. Eddie pulled the three white stones from his jeans pocket and began juggling them.

"If I hadn't borrowed these from your robe," he told Mr. Morgan, "that tour guide would be telling a very different story — wouldn't she!"

"Yes, she would," the sorcerer replied thoughtfully. "A very different story."

"Let's get out of here!" I cried. "I never want to see this tower again."

"I'm starving!" Eddie exclaimed.

I suddenly realized I was starving, too.

"Shall I perform a food spell?" Mr. Morgan suggested.

Eddie and I each let out a loud groan. "I think I've had enough spells to last a lifetime," I said. "How about we go to Burger Palace for some good old twentieth-century hamburgers and fries!"

Add *more*

to your collection . . .

Here's a chilling preview of

PIANO LESSONS CAN BE MURDER

The sad music continued, floating down the dark, narrow stairway to me.

"Who's up there?" I repeated, my voice shaking just a little.

Again, no reply.

I leaned into the darkness, peering up toward the attic. "Mom, is that you? Dad?"

No reply. The melody was so sad, so slow.

Before I even realized what I was doing, I was climbing the stairs. They groaned loudly under my bare feet.

The air grew hot and stuffy as I reached the top of the stairs and stepped into the dark attic.

The piano music surrounded me now. The notes seemed to be coming from all directions at once.

"Who is it?" I demanded in a shrill, high-pitched voice? I guess I was a little scared. "Who's up here?"

Something brushed against my face, and I nearly jumped out of my skin.

It took me a long, shuddering moment to realize it was the light chain.

I pulled it. Pale yellow light spread out over the long, narrow room.

The music stopped.

"Who's up here?" I called, squinting toward the piano against the far wall.

No one.

No one there. No one sitting at the piano.

Silence.

Except for the floorboards creaking under my feet as I walked over to the piano. I stared at it, stared at the keys.

I don't know what I expected to see. I mean, *someone* was playing the piano. *Someone* played it until the exact second the light went on. Where did they go?

I ducked down and searched under the piano.

I know it was stupid, but I wasn't thinking clearly. My heart was pounding really hard, and all kinds of crazy thoughts were spinning through my brain.

I leaned over the piano and examined the keyboard. I thought maybe this was one of those old-fashioned pianos that played by itself. A player piano. You know, like you sometimes see in cartoons.

But it looked like an ordinary piano. I didn't see anything special about it.

I sat down on the bench.

And jumped up.

The piano bench was warm! As if someone had just been sitting on it!

"Whoa!" I cried aloud, staring at the shiny, black bench.

I reached down and felt it. It was definitely warm.

But I reminded myself the whole attic was really warm, much warmer than the rest of the house. The heat seemed to float up here and stay.

I sat back down and waited for my racing heart to return to normal.

What's going on here? I asked myself, turning to stare at the piano. The black wood was polished so well, I could see the reflection of my face staring back at me.

My reflection looked pretty scared.

I lowered my eyes to the keyboard and then hit a few soft notes.

Someone had been playing this piano a few moments ago, I knew.

But how could they have vanished into thin air without me seeing them?

I plunked another note, then another. The sound echoed through the long, empty room.

Then I heard a loud creak. From the bottom of the stairs.

I froze, my hand still on the piano keys.

Another creak. A footstep.

I stood up, surprised to find my legs all trembly.

I listened. I listened so hard, I could hear the air move.

Another footstep. Louder. Closer.

Someone was on the stairs. Someone was climbing to the attic.

Someone was coming for me.

About the Author

R.L. STINE is the author of the series *Fear Street*, *Nightmare Room*, *Give Yourself Goosebumps*, and the phenomenally successful *Goosebumps*. His thrilling teen titles have sold more than 250 million copies internationally — enough to earn him a spot in the *Guinness Book of World Records*! Mr. Stine lives in New York City with his wife, Jane, and his son, Matt.

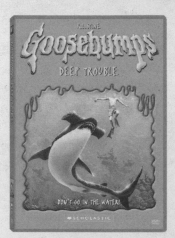

Collect Them All!

Goosebumps®

By R.L. Stine

Each Book $4.99

- ❏ Goosebumps: Abominable Snowman of Pasadena
- ❏ Goosebumps: Attack of the Jack-O-Lanterns
- ❏ Goosebumps: Attack of The Mutant
- ❏ Goosebumps: Bad Hare Day
- ❏ Goosebumps: Barking Ghost
- ❏ Goosebumps: The Beast from the East
- ❏ Goosebumps: Be Careful What You Wish For...
- ❏ Goosebumps: The Cuckoo Clock of Doom
- ❏ Goosebumps: The Curse of Camp Cold Lake
- ❏ Goosebumps: Curse of the Mummy's Tomb
- ❏ Goosebumps: Deep Trouble
- ❏ Goosebumps: Egg Monsters from Mars
- ❏ Goosebumps: Ghost Beach
- ❏ Goosebumps: Ghost Camp
- ❏ Goosebumps: Ghost Next Door
- ❏ Goosebumps: The Girl Who Cried Monster
- ❏ Goosebumps: Go Eat Worms!
- ❏ Goosebumps: The Haunted Mask
- ❏ Goosebumps: The Haunted Mask II
- ❏ Goosebumps: The Headless Ghost
- ❏ Goosebumps: The Horror at Camp Jellyjam
- ❏ Goosebumps: How I Got My Shrunken Head
- ❏ Goosebumps: How to Kill a Monster

- ❏ Goosebumps: It Came from Beneath the Sink!
- ❏ Goosebumps: Lets Get Invisible
- ❏ Goosebumps: Monster Blood
- ❏ Goosebumps: Monster Blood II
- ❏ Goosebumps: A Night in Terror Tower
- ❏ Goosebumps: Night of the Living Dummy
- ❏ Goosebumps: Night of the Living Dummy II
- ❏ Goosebumps: Night of the Living Dummy III
- ❏ Goosebumps: One Day at HorrorLand
- ❏ Goosebumps: Piano Lessons Can Be Murder
- ❏ Goosebumps: Revenge of the Lawn Gnomes
- ❏ Goosebumps: Say Cheese and Die!
- ❏ Goosebumps: Say Cheese and Die — Again!
- ❏ Goosebumps: The Scarecrow Walks at Midnight
- ❏ Goosebumps: Shocker on Shock Street
- ❏ Goosebumps: Stay Out of the Basement
- ❏ Goosebumps: Vampire Breath
- ❏ Goosebumps: Welcome to Camp Nightmare
- ❏ Goosebumps: Welcome to Dead House
- ❏ Goosebumps: The Werewolf of Fever Swamp
- ❏ Goosebumps: Why I'm Afraid of Bees
- ❏ Goosebumps: You Can't Scare Me!

■ SCHOLASTIC

GBKLST0805

Read at Your Own Risk
Goosebumps
By R. L. Stine

____ 0-439-72705-8 **Goosebumps: Attack of the Jack-O-Lanterns**

____ 0-439-66215-X **Goosebumps: Attack of The Mutant**

____ 0-439-66216-8 **Goosebumps: Bad Hare Day**

____ 0-439-66990-1 **Goosebumps: Be Careful What You Wish For**

____ 0-439-72403-1 **Goosebumps: The Beast from the East**

____ 0-439-72404-X **Goosebumps: The Curse of Camp Cold Lake**

____ 0-439-56828-5 **Goosebumps: Deep Trouble**

____ 0-439-56829-3 **Goosebumps: Egg Monsters from Mars**

____ 0-439-56830-7 **Goosebumps: Ghost Beach**

____ 0-439-56831-5 **Goosebumps: Ghost Camp**

____ 0-439-69353-5 **Goosebumps: The Girl Who Cried Monster**

____ 0-439-67114-0 **Goosebumps: Go Eat Worms!**

____ 0-439-67113-2 **Goosebumps: The Haunted Mask II**

____ 0-439-66987-1 **Goosebumps: The Headless Ghost**

____ 0-439-56837-4 **Goosebumps: It Came from Beneath the Sink!**

____ 0-439-66988-X **Goosebumps: Monster Blood II**

____ 0-439-67111-6 **Goosebumps: A Night in Terror Tower**

____ 0-439-57374-2 **Goosebumps: Night of the Living Dummy II**

____ 0-439-66989-8 **Goosebumps: Night of the Living Dummy III**

____ 0-439-56841-2 **Goosebumps: One Day at HorrorLand**

____ 0-439-67112-4 **Goosebumps: Piano Lessons Can Be Murder**

____ 0-439-57375-0 **Goosebumps: Revenge of the Lawn Gnomes**

____ 0-439-56842-0 **Goosebumps: Say Cheese and Die!**

____ 0-439-57361-0 **Goosebumps: Say Cheese and Die—Again!**

____ 0-439-56843-9 **Goosebumps: The Scarecrow Walks at Midnight**

____ 0-439-72706-6 **Goosebumps: Vampire Breath**

____ 0-439-56846-3 **Goosebumps: Welcome to Camp Nightmare**

____ 0-439-56848-X **Goosebumps: The Werewolf of Fever Swamp**

____ 0-439-57365-3 **Goosebumps: You Can't Scare Me!**

____ 0-439-69354-3 **Goosebumps: Why Im Afraid of Bees**

Available Wherever Books Are Sold, or Use This Order Form.

Scholastic Inc., P.O. Box 7502, Jefferson City, MO 65102

Please send me the books I have checked above. I am enclosing $_____ (please add $2.00 to cover shipping and handling). Send check or money order—no cash or C.O.D.s please.

Name_____ Birth date_____

Address_____

City_____ State/Zip_____

Please allow four to six weeks for delivery. Offer good in U.S.A. only. Sorry, mail orders are not available to residents of Canada. Prices subject to change.

SCHOLASTIC